THE
SILVER
SETUP

Richard Blaine

THE SILVER SETUP

A Michael Garrett Mystery

Richard Blaine

First published by Level Best Books/Historia 2022

Copyright © 2022 by Richard Blaine

All rights reserved. No part of this publication may be reproduced, stored or transmitted in any form or by any means, electronic, mechanical, photocopying, recording, scanning, or otherwise without written permission from the publisher. It is illegal to copy this book, post it to a website, or distribute it by any other means without permission.

This novel is entirely a work of fiction. The names, characters and incidents portrayed in it are the work of the author's imagination. Any resemblance to actual persons, living or dead, events or localities is entirely coincidental.

Richard Blaine asserts the moral right to be identified as the author of this work.

Author Photo Credit: Dutch Doscher, dutchdoscher.com

First edition

ISBN: 978-1-68512-216-4

Cover art by Level Best Designs

This book was professionally typeset on Reedsy. Find out more at reedsy.com

Thanks to Ilsa Lund and Aidan Kane

Chapter One

It had started with a missing-persons case. There had been a lot of them since the war, and by 1948 kids were getting pretty restless. This one was the daughter of an average Southern California millionaire. She had gotten mixed up with a bad crowd, left home, left school, and left town. She came east with Arnie Hinson, a cheap hustler with big promises. What he delivered was fleabag hotels, stardom in a couple of stag films, and a world full of junkies. In the City of Brotherly Love, she had found just about everything else.

I had come to Philadelphia to give the deposition that was certain to convict Mannie Floren and the Hinson brothers. The trial had lasted three days, two of them spent waiting, and I was ready to leave the cold city dampness and take a train back home to L.A. The company was no better there, but at least it was warm.

The phone call came early that morning. She wouldn't say how she knew Detective Ed Rawls, but that's how she got my name. She sounded upset and frightened. She said it was imperative that I meet with her, and could I drive out to Lancaster that afternoon? *Imperative.* That sounded like money. I was between cases, and my wallet was looking as empty as an old maid's dance card. I told her there would be expenses for my trip even if I didn't take her case. She agreed. So, I rented a DeSoto and drove west to the town of Lancaster.

It was one of those old industry towns. The clutter of rusting scrap metal and abandoned vehicles lay in too many yards, near too many streets. The homes, rowhouses mostly, seemed huddled together against the cold. Many were freshly painted, as if to deny the encroachment of age. The gray of late winter hung over the streets and blended with the trail of sooty smoke rising from the foundry. People would keep to themselves in a town like this. And they would notice an outsider.

I pulled the DeSoto up to the curb, between a Checker cab and a black Packard coupe, got out, and headed toward Ryan's Tavern. It was a drab little pub, a gathering place for the locals. It was mostly brown-stained clapboard. There were small latticework windows, no curtains, and double doors with brass handles, discolored from years of use. Each door had a square window with a shamrock and the name *Ryan's* in green script lettering. As I approached the door, an old gray dog came over and sniffed my pant leg. Then he made a grumbling noise and sauntered off up the street, unimpressed.

I went in and sat down at the far end of the bar, away from the door. It was a quiet place, long and narrow, with a small section extending across the back past the bar. Everything was clean, but there wasn't much more than the bare essentials. The outer wall was lined with wooden booths, and there were several small tables and straight-backed chairs toward the front. At one of the tables sat four men in work clothes, drinking beer, and huddled over the table talking quietly. They eyed me when I came in. Occasionally, one of them, with a brown leather flyer's jacket draped over the back of his chair, would nod in my direction.

He was wearing dungarees, and a plaid shirt with the sleeves tightly rolled up over an arm that would have made Joe Louis nervous. He had a long chin shaped like the front of a destroyer; it seemed to stand out because his walnut-sized ears were flat, almost pasted to the side of his head. His nose jutted out in the middle of the bridge as if it had been broken, and his forehead sloped up to a forest of dark red hair bathed in Vitalis. He had the look of someone who had thrown a few punches and taken a lot more.

The bartender came over, a round man with a round red face. "Get you something?" he asked.

"Scotch."

He ambled away, then came back carrying a bottle wrapped in an envelope

CHAPTER ONE

of dust. He poured about two inches into a glass and put the bottle down on the bar. I drank it down while he stood back and watched. It wasn't any worse than drinking battery acid from the DeSoto.

"We don't see many strangers in here," he said.

"No wonder if you serve them this."

He grunted and walked away. Reluctantly, I poured another. I sipped this one. It didn't help. Then, as I put down my glass, there she was. She wasn't exactly beautiful, but everyone watched her. She was probably in her early thirties, about five-six, with brown hair and smoldering, deep brown eyes that made you feel you were the only one left in the world.

She was wearing a camel-colored coat with a carefully fastened belt, a filmy, pale blue scarf, and a navy-blue beret angled over her right eye. Her skin was smooth and tanned, and a modest amount of lip rouge almost hid an inviting pout. No one would object to her delicate features. But these all seemed to point to the beginnings of worry lines around the eyes.

"Mr. Garrett?"

"That's right."

"You're punctual," she said. "I like that."

"It's part of the usual service."

"Shall we sit in a booth." The way she said it, there wasn't a question mark at the end.

"Why not? It's your money."

She frowned and walked toward the back corner of the room. We sat down, and she ordered a martini. I decided not to have any more of the Scotch.

"How did you recognize me?" I asked.

"Edward Rawls told me to look for someone tall, with dark hair and eyes and…" She glanced up and then looked quickly down at the table. "And a hat that had been left out in the rain."

I grunted, took off my hat, and dropped it in the booth next to me. "That's Eddie, all right."

The martini came, and she fiddled with the glass for a long while. Finally, she looked up and said, "I don't know how to begin."

I just waited.

"My husband is missing."

I asked the obvious question. "Have you been to the police?"

"Edward says you're someone I can trust." This time there was a hint of a question.

"He and I have worked together several times." I stretched it a little, but not much.

She hesitated. "But I don't know you."

I let out a breath. "All right. My name is Michael Garrett. I'm a licensed private investigator and have been since I was asked to leave the police force some years ago. Something about an attitude problem. I'm forty-two years old. I live in LA. Except for the war, I've lived there most of my life. I never knew my parents. I'm not married, and when I die, there'll be nothing for anyone to inherit. I've been in jail a few times. That's where I met Ed Rawls, about eight years ago. I was on a case; so was he. I'll take most anything but divorce cases. I drink, I smoke, I swear, I like good music and good Scotch. I also like women, but not just fluff in skirts. What I don't like is talking about myself. Now tell me about your husband, Mrs. Stevens."

She smiled. "You're certainly abrupt."

"Yeah. I cry myself to sleep over it."

She hesitated again, then sat back. "I knew Edward ten years ago when he was working in Philadelphia. After he went to Los Angeles, we continued to write." She flushed a little and looked down. "He was a dear friend." There was a slight pause. "I read about you in the Philadelphia paper. You were testifying against those narcotics peddlers. It said you were a private detective from Los Angeles. I wanted someone who wouldn't be familiar in Lancaster, so I took a chance and called Edward."

"Fine. You found your private dick from out of town. Rawls must have told you what I just did, so now you've heard it twice. And you've got a missing husband. Well, the meter's running."

"Please, Mr. Garrett," she said. "Don't be impatient. This is difficult for me."

"Sorry. It's the nature of the job."

She leaned forward and pushed her glass aside. "My husband, Charles

CHAPTER ONE

Stevens, is owner and president of Stevens Associates. His firm owns and operates several businesses in Lancaster, including the Wheelright Foundry. A lot of people in our town work there. He called me from his office two nights ago and said he wouldn't be home for dinner. I haven't seen him or heard from him since then."

By now, it was obvious. "And you haven't been to the police."

"I can't. His position…Charles is well known and respected. And lately, he's even become involved in politics. There are so many people depending on him. If they thought something was wrong…"

"You do, or I wouldn't be here." I finished my drink, put down the glass, and looked into those brown eyes. "Take my advice, Mrs. Stevens. Go to the police."

She reached over and put her hand on my arm. "Please find him, Mr. Garrett. My God, I'm so frightened."

It was thirty bucks a day, plus expenses. So, L.A. could wait a few more days. As I drove away from the pub, I noticed something nagging at me. It was the way you feel when you leave home on a trip, knowing you've forgotten something, but not knowing what. I knew she wasn't telling me everything. That was normal. There had to be more.

Mrs. Stevens had given me a picture of her husband. He looked like the executive she had described—lean, handsome, eyes showing the brutal detachment of the wealthy and powerful. From what she had told me, if Lancaster were a one-horse town, Stevens would own the horse. His family had always had money, but he had made his own fortune. During the Depression, he had bought the Wheelright Foundry for a song. Then, convincing enough people in Congress that Hitler could be a real threat, he obtained a series of government munitions contracts. After the war, Stevens quickly retooled his plant to serve all the firms, large and small, that were beginning to grow again. Business was good. If you couldn't afford to pay him, he would loan you the money to get started.

As Wheelright grew and prospered, so did the town of Lancaster, and in the middle of it all was Charles Stevens, member of the town council, board of education, board of directors at the country club, and prominent in local church activities. He was also a generous donor to every charity, from the Red Cross to the Society to Preserve Your Aunt Minnie's Goldfish. Everybody in town seemed to depend either on Stevens or his money. And now he was missing.

I checked into a small hotel on Central Avenue called the Pilgrim. There wasn't much to it, just a small lobby with a tired potted palm, a seedy-looking red couch, and a front desk. Behind the desk was an elderly, gray-haired woman with a purple-veined nose and breath that smelled of gin. Compared to her, the palm looked like a dozen fresh roses. For a few bucks more than it was worth, she gave me a room that was small and seedy. But it was a place to pour a drink in and flop. I dropped my bag on the bed, went downstairs, and climbed back into the DeSoto.

Mrs. Stevens had given me directions. I drove up Central from the hotel, turned onto West Liberty, and went all the way to the end. The Wheelright foundry was in the northwestern part of town. In fact, it *was* the northwestern part of town. At the end of West Liberty, a chain link fence and a uniformed guard stood at the entrance. I was expected. Mrs. Stevens didn't want anyone to know why I was there, so the line she gave out was that I was investigating an insurance claim, something about missing equipment.

Inside the gate, a large yard with well-worn footpaths was spread out in front of the main plant. The guard directed me along a narrow drive to the right and into a parking area at the end of a smaller building that faced across the yard toward the plant. It was an old building, mostly brick, with tall casement windows and a stark cement cornice projecting out along the top. There was a door marked ADMINISTRATION. I went In.

Inside the narrow-tiled foyer were a half-dozen marble stairs. I could have climbed them if it hadn't been for the kid almost knocking me over. He had close-cropped black hair, pimples, and a full youthful mustache—the kind a cat could lick off. His pale green overalls almost covered his white shirt, but not his yellow bow tie. He stood and blinked at me.

"Do you need a license to wear that outfit?" I asked him.

"What?"

CHAPTER ONE

"Forget it. Just tell me where to find Mr. Stevens's office."

"Upstairs," he said. "Second floor, and to the right." Then he bolted out the door and into the yard. This time I did climb the stairs.

The nameplate on the door said simply, CHARLES STEVENS, PRES. I opened the door and walked into a waiting room. It was somewhat smaller than the Polo Grounds, with light fawn-colored walls and a high dusty-white ceiling. The furnishings were both austere and expensive. Along the front wall were several plush chairs, and on the right was a sofa that seemed as long as a bowling alley. They were all covered in a rich-looking brown leather that didn't invite you to sit on it. Above the sofa was a gilt-framed portrait of a man, with a little gold plaque under it that read, ERNEST WHEELRIGHT, FOUNDER. He looked the part, with neatly trimmed white hair and a beard, a dark suit and vest with a gold watch chain across the front, and an expression to go with a rainy day. He sat in a high-backed chair, with his hands resting on the arms, glaring out like an impatient landlord.

Across the room, a set of deep-red velvet drapes with tassel trim framed a large picture window. Through the window, I could see the foundry. It was like looking at a stage, with the plant forming a backdrop and the people crossing the main yard as actors in a play.

At the far end of the room, a large dark-grained wooden desk with no trim guarded the door to the inner office. A leaf holding a typewriter extended out on the left side, and a hand stuck out under the front. It was a nice hand, with pale, slender fingers and polished nails. The hand kept reaching, as if the desk had dropped something and couldn't quite find it. As I moved closer, the desk said, "Damn." Before I could ask the desk what was wrong, the hand landed on my shoe. Then the desk said, "Harold, don't just stand there. Help me find it."

"Find what?"

"The ribbon. I…" A surprised face looked up from behind the desk. I couldn't tell what she looked like. Most of her face was hidden behind a pair of tortoiseshell glasses. "You're not Harold."

"Nuts. And I was trying so hard."

"I dropped my typewriter ribbon. I was expecting Harold. He always helps me change it."

I gave her a knowing grin. "The lucky dog!"

She stood up and began clutching at the remains of her dignity. "You're not supposed to be here. I mean…"

The outer door opened, and a young man in overalls hurried in. It was the kid from downstairs.

She held up her hand, determined to restore her composure. "Never mind, Harold. I'll take care of it."

But he handed her a folded piece of paper and blurted, "Here." Then he glanced at me, fidgeted a little, and rushed out.

I leaned against the desk. "Your Harold seems like the strong, silent type."

"He's not my Harold. He's just…" She began to blush as she slowly looked down at the note.

"Read your mail," I said. "I'll wait."

I watched her as she read. She was in her early twenties, medium height, with toneless features that might have been scrubbed every hour. Her sandy hair, pulled back in a bun, wouldn't attract much attention. The rest of her wouldn't either. She wore no makeup, and her pencil-thin lips and eyebrows seemed to disappear behind those glasses. Only her gray-green eyes stood out, enlarged by the lenses, appearing very round and moist. She wore a plain, shapeless blue dress and a gray cardigan sweater, covering a figure that probably no one had ever tried to find. Maybe Harold, but I didn't think so.

Slowly, she looked up from the note. "Oh, dear. You're Mr. Garrett?"

"Yes. I'm here to see Mr. Stevens."

She hesitated. "But he's…."

"Not in. I know." It was time to take the lead. "Since you obviously work closely with Mr. Stevens, you must know why I'm here."

She looked at the note again. "It says insurance investigation."

"That's right. And I need some information from his office. So, let's go in and help me find it." I took her arm firmly and ushered her toward the office door. She didn't resist.

We entered and stood in the middle of the room for a minute, just looking. It was smaller than I had expected and designed for privacy. The window

CHAPTER ONE

behind the large mahogany desk was covered with a Venetian blind, so you could let the light in but not be seen from outside. There were three plain wooden chairs in front of the desk. They stood on a dark red carpet with a pile so thick it made you feel as if you were trespassing. The walls, done in a dark paneling, were studded with photographs. Every shot showed Stevens smiling and shaking hands with someone who would be worth at least a column in the local paper. There were congressmen, senators, movie stars, ball players, and the photos were all autographed.

In the far corner to the left, I noticed another door. "Where does that lead?"

"That's Mr. Stevens's private entrance."

I tried the door. It was locked. I turned to the desk. There was nothing but a writing set on top, so I tried the drawers. I found the usual things—pens, pencils, stationery, a folder with notes on production schedules, and more pictures. But the top drawer in the middle was locked too.

I looked up at the girl. By now, she was wearing a worried prim expression. "Mr. Garrett, I don't think Mr. Stevens would like having you go through his desk."

I walked around and stood next to her, and put on my most comforting smile. "You're right. And I know you have a big responsibility. A man's office is very important to his girl Friday. I'll be very careful."

"Well, be sure that you do," she said, getting a little bolder. "But it's not Friday. It's Winnie. Winnie Adams. *Miss* Winnie Adams."

I gave her my best look of disbelief. "You're kidding!"

She reddened, excused herself, and almost fell over a chair on her way out the door. After she left, I picked up a letter opener. It wasn't hard to get the drawer open, but they would need a new opener for the letters from now on.

People tend to have reasons for locking desk drawers. The checkbook was hidden in the back under some envelopes. I thumbed through the stubs. It took a while, maybe a minute, and there it was. Around the middle of every month, an entry showed one hundred dollars to "Cash," with a note reading. "S.L." I returned the checkbook and noticed a book of matches in the corner of the drawer. Printed on the cover was SHADY LODGE MOTEL, ROUTE 12, LANCASTER, PA. On the inside, someone had written the name *Gloria*.

I put the matches in my pocket, shut the drawer, and went out.

People also have reasons for putting names in matchbooks. Miss Winnie Adams gave me directions to Route 12 and the Shady Lodge Motel. She gave me an embarrassed look when I asked her if she knew where the place was. And she acted surprised when I said I wanted to go there.

As I drove through the gate and headed back up West Liberty, a Checker cab fell leisurely in behind me. I drove about six blocks, crossed Main, and turned south onto Central Avenue. The cab did too. It could have been coincidence. For all I knew, a town this size might have more than one taxi. I pulled over to the curb in front of a weather-beaten drugstore, got out, and went across the street.

On the corner was an old tailor shop. It was part of a tired-looking two-story rowhouse that seemed to have all it could do to stand up through another unfriendly winter. The paint was cracked, a dull dark green that could have been war surplus. In front was a picture window with stenciling that read, SOLOMON'S CUSTOM FITS AND ALTERATIONS. Next to the window was a recessed entryway with a grimy glass door. I stepped into the doorway and watched the cab come tentatively up to the corner and stop.

The driver had his window down with his left arm draped casually over the door. The backseat was empty. I saw a flash of dark red hair as the man leaned over, eyeing the DeSoto and the drugstore. He sat idling for a minute, then started slowly around the corner, as if he might be circling the block. I lit a cigarette and waited.

I turned up my collar and tightened the belt on my trench coat against the freezing dampness. It still came through my socks. I was starting to think I was wasting my time when the cab swung back onto Central and nosed up in front of the drugstore again. As I was about to put the arm on him, I heard a tapping on the door behind me. A pear-shaped old man with a mouth that kept moving like the gills of a tropical fish was motioning me inside. The cab driver looked over, saw me, and saw the old man opening the door. Then he turned forward and headed off down Central.

"You're wanting something?" The man stood staring up at me with both

CHAPTER ONE

hands outstretched, his stubby fingers smeared with chalk. There was more chalk smudged on his rumpled dark trousers and vest. He wore a white shirt, open at the collar, sleeves rolled up. The buttons were doing their best to keep the shirt closed over a stomach that hung over his belt like the yolk of an egg falling out of its shell. He had a tape measure draped around a neck that bulged over his shirt collar. His head was hairless, except for a wispy white fringe that hung in sprigs over his ears and eyebrows like untrimmed shrubbery. A pair of half-glasses rested about halfway down his long bulb of a nose, and he peered over them with anxious gray eyes that looked at me as if I were a process server. "Something?" he asked again.

"I think I just missed it." I looked down the street. The cab was gone.

"What?"

"Never mind," I said. "I'm just a tourist."

"Listen." He was wide-eyed. "That suit. I fix it for you."

"It isn't broken."

"Never mind," he said. "I fit you good. But please, mister. You tell Frankie. I got no more money. I'm just a poor tailor. His suits I fix, your suits too. But I can't pay." The hands were reaching for me now. He had my attention.

"So, you can't pay. What's Frankie going to do?"

"You're asking me? Please, I want no trouble."

"You won't get any from me." I paused and casually folded my arms. "Just tell me about Frankie."

His mouth dropped open. He stepped back, almost losing his glasses, his eyes as big as half dollars. "You're not coming in that cab? You're not with Frankie?"

He turned and reeled back into his shop and leaned with both hands on a counter that faced out toward the street. "My mouth I should be shutting."

"So, this Frankie was driving the cab. And he's shaking you down?"

"So, who's asking?" He squinted up at me, licking his lips.

I flashed him my California ID just long enough to make him think it meant something in Pennsylvania.

"So, you're a policeman?" he asked.

"Private," I said. "The name is Garrett. Now, who is Frankie, and how much is he taking?"

He threw up his hands, gazed at the ceiling, then let his hands drop. "Frankie Bell. Each week he's coming and taking twenty dollars. One week no twenty, and next day my window is smashed." He motioned in that direction and leaned against the counter. "You're what's called a shamus?" For the first time, there was a tired smile.

"Why don't you go to the police?" I asked. That was always a good question.

"The police I'm telling, and my window is breaking. Maybe it's me next time." He stood up again and touched my arm. "Mister…Mister Garrett. I'm an old man. What can I do? It's not just Frankie. It's his people. It's this neighborhood, this town. Everybody is afraid. One old man… His hands fell to his sides, and he stared at his shoes.

"How many is he taking from?"

"I don't know. Most of the neighborhood, I think. People don't talk about it much."

"Look," I said. "I'm just passing through. I have a client, and I only take one case at a time. But that guy was on my tail, and I want to know why. He's squeezing you for protection money, and he saw me come in here. Chances are you'll hear about it. When does he come to collect?"

He shoved his hands into his pockets, and chalk dust floated across the room. He stared out at the street and began talking wistfully, almost to himself.

"Three years now since my Sophie's gone. Always she was saying. 'Sol, you must stand up and tell, like a mensch. Never mind other people.' So, I guess now I must stand up and tell."

He stood erect, breathed deeply, and pulled off his glasses, sliding them into his vest pocket. "Friday, he comes. That's tomorrow. About noon. He takes the money. Sometimes he brings clothes, suits, jackets, even shirts. I fix them up like he tells me. Only…only they're not his."

"You're fitting clothes for somebody who doesn't come in here?"

"It's not just *somebody* I'm fitting," he said. "It's the one they call Silver. Frankie works for him, they say. About Silver, you don't ask."

I shrugged. "All right, Mr. Solomon. I'll be here tomorrow, around noon.

CHAPTER ONE

And we'll talk to Frankie Bell."

He squeezed his hands together, with his fingers interlocked, and his brow wrinkled all the way back to his shirt collar. "You're a young man. Lots of life you have left. Be careful."

I pressed his hand and went back to the car, and headed on down Central. L.A. had nothing on this town. The big guys pick on the little ones wherever you are. It took me about ten minutes to drive down Route 12 and find the exit. It was almost dark when I turned off the highway and saw the sign.

Chapter Two

Shady Lodge was a rustic-looking motel. Behind a circular drive there was an ordinary two-story white house with blue trim. The roof was gabled across the front. The windows had filmy white curtains, all pulled closed. In front, a set of neatly rounded evergreens led up to a small porch with two slender white columns. On one was a sign that said OFFICE.

Next to the house, a string of little cabins meandered through some trees along the edge of a small creek. Lots of privacy at Shady Lodge. Each cabin was a miniature replica of the main house, and each one looked occupied. Several cars were parked along the drive. Nothing fancy, just a small fleet of Buicks, Packards, and Cadillacs.

I went into the main house. There was a desk with the usual disinterested clerk behind it, a frail-looking character with blond hair parted in the middle, and a William Powell mustache. I told him I was looking for a guy, and he gave me a quizzical smirk. You'd think I had just asked a mortician where to find the office party. For a fin, he admitted that the man in the picture I flashed him was staying in Number Seven. For another five, he managed to find an extra key. When I took it, he smirked again.

I drove down to the end and stopped in front of the last cabin. There was no answer when I knocked, so I let myself in. It was just one room, with a small gas heater in the corner and two doors on the far wall behind the bed. One stood open, showing an empty closet. On the right, opposite the metal bed, was a plain wooden dresser with a small mirror hanging on the wall above. Next to the bed was a wooden nightstand holding a brass reading lamp, a phone, and a notepad with the corners curled up.

CHAPTER TWO

He was stretched out on the bed, shoes off and a newspaper in his lap. He might have been dozing, except for the bullet hole in his chest. From the way he didn't move, there was no doubt that Mrs. Stevens was now a widow. His suit jacket and tie were neatly folded over a chair next to the nightstand, and his shoes were sitting neatly side by side at the end of the bed. As I moved closer, I could see his right hand clutching a small pistol, probably a .32 caliber. My guess was one shot through the heart fired from very close range. The brownish powder burns on his shirt blended with a crusted crimson where the blood had run down and collected across his waist. Even dead, Charles Stevens had a certain look of authority. But his shallow stare was dry and clouded, and he lay very still and silent.

A stale sweet smell hung in the air, like burnt flowers. I went into the bathroom and used my fountain pen to open the cabinet. It was all there: razor, hair tonic, toothbrush. Obviously, he intended to die well-groomed. Under the sink was a wastebasket with a large pile of ashes burying a single cigarette butt on the bottom, and there was more of the sweet burning smell. Among the ashes was a small piece of pale blue paper, wadded tightly into a ball. I went back out front and quietly closed the door, being careful not to touch anything. This wasn't what I'd had in mind that morning when I'd agreed to drive out and meet Mrs. Stevens.

I went back to the main office. The clerk was still there, sitting behind the desk, reading a movie magazine. I tossed the key on the desk, and he casually crossed one leg over the other. He gave me another smirk. "Your guy didn't have anything for you, huh?"

I was ready to make him eat it. "You can't have much fun with a stiff."

His face went blank. He stood up.

"Before I have you call the police, I want my ten bucks' worth. Tell me what was going on in Number Seven."

His eyelids fluttered. "What do you mean, stiff? I didn't…nobody was…who the hell are you?"

"I thought I might buy the place, but there's a mess in one of your cabins."

Now he frowned. The smirk looked better. "Okay, wise guy, dust. Beat it."

"Look," I said. "There's a body in Seven. And there was dope there.

Somebody brought it in or got it here. You want to tell me or wait for the cops? I'm cold and impatient, so make up your mind."

He just stared at me with his mouth hanging open. Then he shuffled sideways a little and looked at the window, biting his lip. "Look, mister, all I do is answer the phone and hand out keys. I don't know anything."

"Let me guess. The guy in Seven checked in without any luggage, right?"

His eyebrows went up. "Well, yeah. I mean, right, no luggage."

"And you just answer the phone for some swell girls who only want to work in a nice homey place, right?" I watched his jaw tighten. "Who was working Number Seven?"

His breath came out slowly, and he leaned forward, both hands on the desk. "You didn't get it here, all right? Her name's Gloria. Gloria Tempest. That's all I know."

"Where does she live?"

"I don't know. None of them tell me that. Most of them don't even talk to me. But she works at the Silver Club. A waitress, I think."

"How will I know her?"

"She's a blonde." He looked down toward the desk and spoke quietly. "You'll know her all right."

"Thanks," I said. "Now call the cops."

I went outside and stood on the porch. I wanted to get some air that didn't make me feel dirty just from breathing. It was dark now, and a quiet cold rain was falling. I was about to light a cigarette when I heard a car being slammed into gear, the tires screeching. At the far end of the driveway, I saw a Checker cab turn out onto the road and head back toward Route 12, making a swishing sound on the wet pavement. I jumped into the DeSoto and felt the car lurch onto the road like an overweight bullfrog. I leaned forward, peering through the rain as I nosed down the drive, but all I could see were taillights. By the time I got to the highway, I couldn't even see them. Somehow, this just wasn't my night. I turned the car around and drove back to the motel.

I pulled up in front of Number Seven again, next to a black-and-white patrol car, and saw the lights on in the cabin. Lancaster's finest hadn't taken

CHAPTER TWO

long. I went to the door, opened it, and went in. There were two of them, large economy size. And the kid from the desk was there. When he saw me, he pointed toward me.

"That's him. That's the guy that rousted me."

One of them came over and stuck a nose the size of a golf ball in my face. He had a puffy face with watery blue eyes and brown hair. His brown hat was set back on his head, his trench coat was open over a brown suit, and he wore brogans the size of shoe boxes. I thought if he stood too close to the gas heater, his breath might ignite the room.

"Moran," he snarled at me. "Sergeant Moran. Who the hell are you?"

I looked at the bed. Stevens was still there, staring silently at the whole thing.

"Well?" Moran was getting impatient.

I glanced over at the kid. "Fuller Brush man."

Moran stepped back. "Oh, a wise guy." He smiled at the kid. "That's all, Ralph. Beat It." Ralph ducked his head, went out, and quickly shut the door. I could hear his feet on the gravel outside, running back toward the main house.

Now Moran was smiling at me. "Ralph keeps a quiet place. He says you pushed him around."

"Did Ralph show you the bruises?"

He looked me in the eye, still smiling. But he spoke to his partner. "Ferris, see if he's carrying heat."

Ferris was tall and thin, with large boney hands and a face that didn't budge. He came over and patted me down. It was like taking a trip through a meat grinder. He pulled out my wallet and handed it to Moran. "Just this," he said with a surly nasal whine.

"Sorry," I said. "I left my burglar tools at home."

Moran chuckled and nodded to Ferris. Then a fist the size of a basketball landed just above my right kidney. My knees buckled, and I almost went down. I struggled up, wondering where all the air went. Moran thumbed through my wallet. Then he stepped close and put that nose in my face again.

"Well, Mr. Garrett. Mr. California-private-investigator. Mr. out-of-town snoop. Who the hell invited you?"

"Nobody. I came here for my health. This is a great place for rheumatism."

"Look, punk," he growled. "We take care of things here ourselves. We don't need no foreign peepers."

I looked toward the bed, then I looked back at Moran. "Yeah," I said. "Nice work."

"Button up," he snapped, teeth bared. "Lucky for you, it looks like suicide. But I still wanna know what you're doing here."

Ferris tightened his grip on my arm. "Sure, I'm lucky. Only, tell Dr. Watson here to lay off."

"Okay, Jack." Moran looked at Ferris. "Take him out to the car." Then he smiled again. "Let's sweat him a little."

So, they gave me a free ride to the Lancaster police station. It was about as warm and friendly as any other jail. I spent a couple of hours with my rump on a hard wooden chair, with Moran yelling and pacing around the room. Finally, a uniformed officer came in and told him that Lieutenant Wells wanted to see me. Moran buttoned his vest and announced, "All right, Garrett. You're gonna see the lieutenant. Let's go."

He led me down to the end of a narrow corridor and into an office at the corner of the building. The plaster walls, painted a light green, were covered with a network of fine cracks, and some of the paint had started to chip. There was a large wooden desk in the corner by the windows, with two more hard-looking wooden chairs in front. In the far corner, away from the windows, was a dusty metal filing cabinet. Cops' offices never are much.

Moran pushed me into one of the chairs. "He's all yours, Lieutenant." Then he turned and went out.

Lieutenant Wells was sitting behind the desk, studying the contents of a manila folder. He said nothing, and I sat there for almost five minutes listening to the rain patter on the windows. He was a slender man with black hair and angular features. There were deep furrows in his pale forehead, and his thin black eyebrows curved down toward his ears. And he was showing the stubble of a very dark beard. He could have been thirty or fifty.

CHAPTER TWO

He was wearing two-thirds of a navy-blue suit. The jacket was hung over the back of his chair. His vest was open, and he had on a white shirt, sleeves buttoned, and a maroon tie. In front of him on the desk were a dark green blotter and a telephone, with a small desk lamp to his left. To his right was a framed photograph of a blonde, domestic-looking lady behind two small dark-haired boys. Even cops have families.

"Garrett, isn't it?" He glanced across the desk at me without moving. I just stared at him, and he put the folder down on the desk. "Moran says you haven't exactly been cooperative."

"And here I thought we were getting along just fine."

He turned toward me in his chair. "From what I read about the Hinson trial, I'd say you don't get along with anybody. I thought after the trial was finished in Philadelphia, you'd be on your way back to L.A. What are you doing in Lancaster?"

"I already told your boys. I came here for my health."

He leaned forward in his chair, the furrows getting deeper.

"Never mind," I said. It wasn't funny a second time. "I'm here on a case."

"Who hired you?"

"Lieutenant, I'm sure that even in Lancaster, there's such a thing as a client's privacy."

"Look, Garrett," he said quietly, deliberately. "We're a small town. But we get upset when a prominent citizen shows up dead, and it turns out he was being shadowed by a private eye from the other side of the country. Even if it was suicide, that doesn't mean you can waltz in and out of town and not clear it with us. Now, who's your client?"

I lit a cigarette and looked at him. "I guess it doesn't matter now. Mrs. Stevens hired me to find her husband. He'd been missing for a couple of days, and she wanted someone who wouldn't attract attention to look for him. Only around here, I'm about as inconspicuous as Fred Astaire on top of a flagpole."

"How did you know where to find Charles Stevens?"

"I didn't. I found the name and address of Shady Lodge locked away in his office. It was worth a try. When I got there, he was already dead. But what makes you so sure be killed himself?"

He picked up a pencil and began tapping it on the blotter. "What else could it be? He was shot at close range. He was holding the weapon. There were no other prints, no signs of a struggle. And from what we can tell, the only visitor he had was you."

"Sure," I said. "It happens all the time. A guy decides to commit suicide, so he goes to a motel, spreads out the paper, and shoots himself smack in the middle of the sports section."

Wells put the pencil down and folded his hands. "All right, I'll admit that Shady Lodge is a strange place to find Charles Stevens, alive or dead. We've been watching it for a long time, and we know about the girls and the dope. But every time we go in, all we find are tourists. It's a cinch bet that Silver's running the place, but we just can't prove it."

"Silver?"

He looked at my cigarette. "Can you spare one of those?"

I shook one out of the pack and gave It to him. He lit it, leaned back in his chair, and with one breath, sent up a cloud that covered the ceiling. He studied the cloud for a while. Then he began to recite, like a guy who's been rehearsing for a long time.

"Santino 'Silver' Manelli. Came to this country in 1926, settled in Philadelphia, and went to work right away as a collector and button man for the mob. In eighteen months, he had taken over most of the downtown streets. No shopkeeper could stay open, no fruit peddler could even push his cart down the sidewalk without paying protection money to Manelli. He moved up fast, and by 1931 he was number-two man in an empire as big as any on the East Coast. By 1940 he was running it all. Then he branched out into gambling, numbers, prostitution, and narcotics. Toward the end of the War, when the Feds started putting the heat on in Philly, he moved his operation to Lancaster. He left Joe Hinson minding the store, but he went on calling the action from out here. I think you know Hinson?"

"Yeah." I snorted. "And his brother Arnie. I tracked him all the way to Philly, looking for the daughter of a client."

He nodded and went on. "After a while, Joe decided he wanted to run

CHAPTER TWO

things himself. He hired a torpedo named Spencer and then sent word to Manelli that he wanted a meeting to talk about territory. Next day we found Spencer divided up in the trunks of three different cars. One was over in Jersey. Joe backed down, but the word was already out about trouble in the organization. Mannie Floren, a Chicago trigger, went to Manelli and told him he wanted Hinson's job. He said he could control the streets, build up the take, and quiet Hinson. That made Joe mad, and he was still powerful in town. But by then, Manelli controlled most of the state and who-knows-what outside. He decided just to sit back here and let the two of them fight it out. Whatever happened, he couldn't lose. That's when you showed up."

"My usual good timing," I said. "Manelli sounds like a real charmer. What does he do here?"

Wells leaned over and flicked his ashes into a wastebasket next to his desk, the same one I had been using. "Nothing we can pin on him. He keeps to himself. Spends most of his time at his club. The Silver Club. Get it? People hardly ever see him outside. He even has his food brought in."

"And his clothes," I muttered, remembering what Solomon had said.

"Who knows? Nobody even knows how old he is. He's never been in jail. He's been picked up once or twice, but never booked, never served time." He stubbed out his cigarette in the wastebasket and put both hands flat on the blotter. Then he looked up at me, his eyebrows seeming to sag. "So, what have I got? I know what's going on out at Shady Lodge, but I can't prove it. I know the place is connected to Manelli, but I can't prove that. I have Charles Stevens dead in a cabin, holding the gun, and, except for you, nothing's out of place. There's nowhere I can go with it."

"Are you sure Stevens was alone?"

He nodded. "As sure as I can be. We checked with the clerk." Then the furrows eased, and a smile started. "Whatever you gave Ralph, it wasn't enough."

"It usually isn't," I shrugged. "Listen, Ralph is so busy looking the other way, he could miss an elephant on his porch."

"Maybe." Wells stood up. "But I've got no reason to doubt him. Anyway, it's not your worry. You can go."

"So that's it? You're just going to drop it?"

"I'll talk with Mrs. Stevens, of course. Maybe I can pick up something about why her husband was at Shady Lodge. But I don't expect much. A lot of people go there, and we both know why. Sure, they don't advertise it, but they go. What makes Stevens any different?"

"One difference is he's dead." Now I stood up. "Look, let me talk to Mrs. Stevens first. She's still my client. I owe her that much."

He put his hands in his pockets and exhaled heavily. "All right. I'll wait until the morning."

"Thanks." I headed for the door.

"Garrett." I stopped and looked around. Wells was back at his desk playing with his pencil. "I don't work the way Moran does. I figure you're smart enough to know that. But don't cross the line on me. Just see your client and then go home. Get it?"

I turned and went out without saying anything. I got it.

The desk sergeant gave me directions, and I got back into the DeSoto. It was starting to feel like home. I headed up Main and turned east onto Flint. This time I didn't see anything in the mirror. I drove out to the suburbs, went from Flint to Halsey Road, and then onto Crestwood Drive. As I turned onto Crestwood, I inspected the houses; they were sedate, mature, probably like the people in them. It was a neighborhood of second, maybe third-generation wealth—the kind those people take for granted and don't try to display, but you can still see it.

I turned in at number seventeen. There were two brick pillars at the end of a driveway that wandered through a handful of tall trees. The modest mansion couldn't have had more than thirty rooms. The front was white shingle siding with black trim and black shutters framing windows the size of parking spaces. The black tiled roof was bordered by eaves with black painted gutters. A small stretch of brick stairs led up to the front door through a spread of shrubbery that must have kept four gardeners busy all year. The brick in front of the door was formed into a terrace, with wrought-iron railings on the sides, also black. And on the black painted door was a shiny brass knocker with a large round knob in the middle.

CHAPTER TWO

Just past the front door, the driveway ended in a small parking area. I left the car and went up the brick stairs. The terrace was covered by a pair of floodlights that made it seem like a stage. I pounded the knob against the door, getting a prosperous clank, stepped back, and tucked in my trench coat. Standing there in the rain, I felt like a school kid going to see the principal. As I was reaching for the knob again, a tall thin man in a white jacket opened the door. He was about sixty, with thin sandy hair, baggy green eyes, and a squared-off mouth and chin. My hand was still reaching in his direction. He looked at it, then looked at me, with only a little indulgence.

"Yes, sir?"

"Can't you people afford a doorbell?" I put my hand back in my pocket.

He looked me over from hat to heels. Then his gaze turned sour, as if I had just spat on his shoe. "I beg your pardon?"

"Skip it. I'm here to see Mrs. Stevens."

His expression became a little more settled. "She's retired, sir."

"Well, unretire her. My name's Garrett. She hired me this afternoon to find her husband."

"Very well, sir," he said, without much interest. "If you would care to wait for a moment, I'll ask if Mrs. Stevens will see you, sir."

"Fine," I said. "I'll just stand out here in the rain."

"Indeed, sir." His lips tightened, and he gave me an impatient look. Then he slowly moved aside and held the door open. I went in.

I stood in an entrance hall that would have made the Astors proud. The marble floor stretched about thirty feet to a flight of stairs that wound up and around to the left. It ended at an open hallway on the second floor. A crystal chandelier hung down into the curve of the stairway that would take at least a week to dust. Any minute I expected Vivien Leigh to come drifting down, ready to greet Clark Gable.

"If you'll wait here a moment, sir, I'll inquire of Mrs. Stevens."

"Leave a trail of crumbs so you can find your way back."

He paused as if he wanted to say something. Then he turned and went slowly up the stairs. I walked into the middle of the hall and looked around. On the wall to the right was a deep red tapestry with a picture of a fat old

Chinese guy stretched out on some pillows. He was sucking on a hose that snaked across his belly and ran into a wide flask with a pipe bowl on top. Three women in kimonos were kneeling on the floor by his feet. They seemed to be admiring him. I wasn't sure why. In front of the tapestry was a wooden stand, an umbrella angled in it with beads of water running off. Next to the stand was a small table with a vase of fresh carnations. I took off my hat and put it on the table, and turned around. On the opposite wall was a mirror that went from floor to ceiling. It didn't do much for me. I straightened my tie. Then I straightened it again.

The old man came back down the stairs. "Mrs. Stevens will see you, sir. You may wait in the drawing room."

"Aren't you afraid I might make a mess on the carpet?"

"Sir." He raised one eyebrow. "I find your manner disturbing."

"Yeah. I'm not crazy about it, either. It came with the suit."

He grunted. "The drawing room is across the hall, sir." He pointed to a doorway just past the mirror. Then he picked up my hat. "And your coat, sir?" I peeled off my dripping trench coat and gave it to him. He walked away, looking as if I'd just handed him a dead cat.

I found the drawing room. It wasn't that hard. I just hiked my way across the hall and into a room the size of a train station. The walls were papered in a pastel blue with white flowers. By the door was a half-acre oriental rug that covered about a third of the room. On both sides of the door were bookcases filled with classics—Homer, Shakespeare, Donne, Hardy, Thoreau. A layer of dust suggested they hadn't been read in a while. Beyond the rug, I saw the back of a sofa. It was a dark-blue print with more white flowers. I moved up behind it and saw two stately chairs, covered in still more blue fabric, and a coffee table with a glass top sitting in front of the sofa. They all faced the fireplace at the end of the room. Above the mantel was a life-size portrait of Charles Stevens sitting by a desk. He stared out silently, the same way I saw him at Shady Lodge.

"Mr. Garrett." I turned and saw Mrs. Stevens enter the room. She had on a creamy white dressing gown with squared shoulders and a sash. Her casually brushed brown hair drifted down over her right shoulder, giving her a soft look. But her deep brown eyes were all business. As she moved toward me, I could see that she wore less makeup than before. The pout of her lower lip was more obvious. She looked completely composed, yet somehow fragile, vulnerable.

"Rogers said that an ill-tempered man named Garrett insisted on seeing me. Have you found my husband?"

Before I could answer, Rogers appeared at the door. "Will there be anything, madam?"

She turned back to me. "Mr. Garrett, would you like some brandy?"

"Good idea," I said. "It's been a cold, wet night. Why don't you have some too?"

Rogers disappeared and returned almost immediately, carrying a tray with a decanter and two glasses. He put the tray down on the coffee table and looked at Mrs. Stevens. "Good night, madam."

"Good night, Rogers." As he left, she began to pour the brandy, then she nodded at me. "Please sit down, Mr. Garrett."

I settled down onto the sofa. It was almost like being swallowed. Next, she handed me a glass, and I took a deep slug. It burned, but not enough.

"Now, about my husband?" She nestled down on the sofa next to me, blinking expectantly.

"Mrs. Stevens, I'm afraid I have some very bad news." She stared at me. There was never an easy way to do this. "Your husband is dead."

She continued to stare, idly playing with her glass. "But…but…."

"I found him at Shady Lodge. It appears that he shot himself."

She leaned over and very deliberately placed her glass on the coffee table. Then she stood up and walked over to the fireplace, and put both hands on the mantel. I could see them trembling. After a long moment, she turned around very slowly, a little unsteady. "Charles is dead?"

I got up and went around the coffee table, and stood next to her. "I saw him. He's dead."

She rubbed her hands together, her eyes whipping from side to side, struggling to hold her poise. "I think you said something about Shady Lodge?"

"Listen, Mrs. Stevens." I put my hand on her arm. "I know this is hard on you, and I'm sorry. But a very efficient police lieutenant named Wells is going to be here tomorrow morning with a lot of questions. It might be easier to take if you go over them with me first."

She inhaled deeply and slowly let it out. "Thank you, Mr. Garrett. I'll be all right."

"Wells believes your husband took his own life. Do you know of any reason why he would?"

"No." She paused. "Well, maybe. I don't know. He wasn't himself lately. He spoke of business reversals. And he talked about...about getting out. I thought...I don't know."

"Getting out?"

"Well, I thought he meant getting out of his businesses. I had no idea."

"Mrs. Stevens, I have to ask. Your marriage. Were you and your husband getting along?"

She breathed deeply and turned back toward the fireplace. "Mr. Garrett, I won't deceive you." She looked down. "No, I won't deceive myself." She straightened and looked at me. "All married couples have their problems. Charles and I were no different. Lately, I'm afraid things had gotten worse between us. I told myself that it was the strain of his business. But I suppose I was partly responsible. I couldn't seem to make him happy. Oh, dear." She suddenly looked startled. "I just remembered. Charles had taken to coming in very late several nights a week. Sometimes he would be out all night. He said he was at the country club. Could he have been going there, to that dreadful place? Oh, I feel so much to blame." She put up her hand and stifled a sob. I led her back to the sofa and waited for a minute.

"Mrs. Stevens, do you know a Gloria Tempest?"

She shook her head.

"Did your husband ever mention a man named Manelli?"

She blinked. "Why no. I mean…. Well, I've heard the name. I've read about him in the newspapers. But Charles never said anything about him."

"What about Frankie Bell?"

"No," she said again. "Never."

"Mrs. Stevens, this won't be easy to take." I held both of her arms. "I don't

CHAPTER TWO

believe your husband committed suicide. I think he was murdered."

Her jaw dropped, and she blinked again. "But why? How could you think that?"

"From the look of the place where he was. He was a meticulous man, organized, used to running things. He wouldn't give up everything he'd built that way. I found his toilet articles neatly lined up in the bathroom. And he had his suit and his shoes laid out neatly, as if he intended to use them again. A man who's going to kill himself isn't neat. What's more, I don't think Wells really believes the suicide angle, either. He's just stuck behind his badge."

Her lower lip began to quiver, and she put her hand up to her mouth. She looked like a lost kitten, shaking from the cold.

"When I take a case," I went on, "I like to see it through. And I've got some unfinished business here. So, I want you to tell Wells that you're keeping me on. Just say it's to tie up loose ends."

"Oh." She exhaled heavily. Her eyes rolled back in her head, and she slumped forward into my shoulder. I lifted her legs onto the sofa and started to look for Rogers. There was a button by the door, so I thumbed it hard. Rogers came down the stairs, his coat off and his tie loosened.

"Mrs. Stevens has fainted. Do you have any smelling salts?"

"Yes, sir." He hurried back upstairs.

I went back to the drawing room. Rogers didn't waste any time. He and a hatchet-faced old lady in a maid's uniform came in right away. He handed me a small bottle. I went over to the sofa, uncapped the bottle, and held it under Mrs. Stevens's nose. She flinched and shook her head to the side. Then she started to groan.

"She'll be all right," I said. "She just needs to rest."

She put up her hand. "Mr. Garrett." I leaned over. "Please help me upstairs."

I picked her up. She seemed to weigh almost nothing. I looked at Rogers. "Point me to the bedroom."

He hesitated, then turned. "This way, sir." I followed him, and hatchet-face followed me. We went upstairs and into a bedroom at the end of the hall. It had the usual frills and a four-poster bed that could sleep six.

Rogers spoke to the old lady. "Martha, turn down the bed, please."

She glowered at him and then pulled off the spread and angled open the blanket and top sheet.

I laid Mrs. Stevens down, tucking her feet under the covers. She had her arms around my neck now, and she kept them there. I started to loosen them, but she opened her eyes and pulled me down so that my nose was almost in her ear. "Please," she whispered. "Please."

I pulled her arms off my neck and straightened up. Her gown had fallen open, exposing a length of thigh that almost made my heart stop. I pulled the blanket up to her chin and leaned over again. "Tell Wells I'm staying."

"Yes," she murmured. "Stay." She turned her head and drifted off.

I stood up again. Rogers and Martha were both staring at me. "Let her sleep," I said. "Tell her I'll talk with her tomorrow."

They looked at each other, then Rogers looked at me. "Yes, sir. I'll show you out, sir."

"Never mind. I know where out is."

I went downstairs with Rogers trailing behind. Somehow, he had already gotten my hat and coat, so I thanked him and went outside. I stood on the porch for a minute. The rain had stopped. I got into the car and drove back downtown.

On my way back to the hotel, I stopped at an all-night liquor store with a sleepy old geezer behind the counter. I bought a bottle of Old Kentucky. It didn't look like much, but I thought it would do the job. When I got to my room, I poured about three ounces into a glass and gulped it down. Then I poured some more and sat on the bed, and looked at my watch. It was close to midnight when I picked up the phone, dialed the Operator, and asked for long distance.

There was a buzz and then a click on the other end. "Yeah?"

"Eddie. It's Garrett."

He chuckled. "I thought you'd be calling, chum. I told Lenore you're an okay shamus. So, try to behave."

"So, it's 'Lenore,' is it?"

"Listen," he grumbled. "That was ten years ago when I was on the force in Philly. Her name was Lenore Parker then. We had something started, but

CHAPTER TWO

then she met this guy, Stevens. It didn't take a Quiz Kid to see that he was going places. He had money, power, prestige. I couldn't compete, so I came out here."

"Well, he's no competition now. He's dead. The cops are saying suicide. I say murder."

"My God." He paused. "How's Lenore taking it?"

"How do you think?"

"Look, I haven't seen her in ten years, but she was alright. Try to look out for her. Okay?"

I grunted. "Sure. Just like your maiden aunt. You heard of a hood named Manelli?"

"Jesus, he's in it? That's a real bad egg. Watch out for your ass."

"How about a cop named Wells?"

"Yeah, I know him. Tough, but honest."

"What about Stevens? Know anything about his business operation?"

"Not much, except he seemed to have the Midas touch. Everything he went near turned to big bucks. I'll dig for you a little and see what I can find out." Then his voice took on a more cautious tone. "On second thought, maybe you better just leave things to Wells."

"Are you kidding? I'm having such a swell time. Tomorrow I'm even going out to see my tailor."

"Christ, Garrett. Be serious. Those guys play for keeps."

"That's the only way."

"All right. All right. Nobody can tell you anything. Keep in touch."

"Sleep tight, Eddie." I hung up the phone and finished my drink. Then I stretched out on the bed, thinking about getting back to L.A. After a while, I poured some more of the Old Kentucky. I held up the glass, looked at It for a minute, and drained it with a couple of swallows.

Chapter Three

It was a rural scene, and I was standing under a tree. It was peaceful there, and a church bell was ringing. But the bell became insistent. It grew louder. It became the bell in a firehouse, pulsing, clanging, telling me to move. I rolled over. It was the telephone.

"Yeah. What is it?" I was still standing under the tree, mad at the fire chief.

"Mr. Garrett? This is Winnie Adams."

"Who? Oh, yeah. Wait a minute." I rolled over, sat up, and tried to shake my head clear. "Hello, Winnie. What is it?"

"Mr. Garrett, I know you're here on an important investigation. But I wish you'd tell Mr. Bell to be more careful."

"What bell? What are you talking about?" I'm always at my best first thing in the morning.

"Mr. Bell," she said. "You must know him. He told me that he's working with you, and he needed something from Mr. Stevens's office, just the way you did."

"Bell, huh? What something?"

"I don't know. But I let him in. And Mr. Garrett, the office. It's a mess. He just tore everything to pieces. I know Mr. Stevens will want your company to pay for the damages."

"Is he still there?"

"Mr. Bell? No," she said. "He left about ten minutes ago. Mr. Stevens will be furious."

"Maybe not. Winnie, what time is it?"

"It's quarter to nine."

CHAPTER THREE

"Look, I'll be there in half…. No, make that an hour. Don't touch anything."

"Touch anything," she blurted. "If Mr. Stevens sees this…Mr. Garrett, I have to clean up everything."

"Did Bell find what he was looking for?"

"I don't think so. He seemed very upset when he left here."

"All right. Clean up if you want. I'll be there in an hour."

I pushed down the receiver. While I still had the phone, I reached for my wallet, pulled out a number, and dialed. There was barely the beginning of a buzz on the other end.

"Stevens' residence."

"Rogers, this is Garrett. Let me talk to Mrs. Stevens."

"I'm sorry, sir," he droned. "Mrs. Stevens can't come to the phone. The doctor was here. She's been sedated."

"What about Lieutenant Wells?"

"Why, yes, sir. He was here early this morning. Quite impertinent, I might say. Insisted on questioning Mrs. Stevens. He was rather annoyed that she couldn't see him."

"Then you know about Mr. Stevens?"

He caught his breath. "Yes, sir. After you left last night, I looked in on Mrs. Stevens to see if she was all right. She was still awake, and she told me about poor Mr. Charles." I could hear him clucking through his teeth as he shook his head. "Such a tragedy. I called the station right away and spoke to Lieutenant Wells. He already knew what had happened. And he said he would be here to see Mrs. Stevens in the morning. By the way, sir. I took the liberty of telling the lieutenant that you would be staying on. He said that he would like to speak with you."

"I'm sure he would. Like the bouncer in a pool hall."

"Sir?"

"Never mind. Did Wells say what he wanted?"

"No, sir. He only asked about Mr. Charles." He clucked again. "It's simply dreadful. I told Martha. She's quite upset."

"Well, I'm sure you handled it like a trooper."

"Thank you, sir," he puffed.

"Tell Mrs. Stevens I'll see her this afternoon."

"Yes, sir." He hung up.

I struggled out of bed, took a lukewarm shower, shaved, and dressed. Then I went out and got some breakfast at a small cafeteria across the street from the hotel. I had lukewarm coffee, toast, and scrambled eggs. The eggs were lukewarm too. I went outside and climbed into the DeSoto, and headed for the foundry. No sign this time of the Checker cab.

It was another drab day, raw and damp. A misty film started to form on the windshield, not enough for wipers, but enough to make things look clouded, distant. I drove through Lancaster's business district. The store windows were all coated with a brownish scum, a residue of the winter. Along the curbs were occasional lingering mounds of grimy snow and ice. The whole scene might have been painted by Norman Rockwell with a hangover.

It was business as usual at the foundry. The same people were trudging across the same yard, the same characters on the same stage. The guard pointed me to the same parking area, and I climbed the same stairs and went into Stevens's office. The office wasn't the same.

The plush chairs and sofa had all been pulled out, away from the wall. The cushions were strewn around the room, each one slit open, with the stuffing spilling out. There were gobs of it all over the floor. The arms and backs of the furniture had all been sliced, and the leather stripped back. And there was more stuffing. It might take the town sanitation truck to clean it up.

I stepped into the middle of the room and looked at the red velvet drapes. They were wrinkled and twisted, as if someone had tried to wring water out of them. I turned and looked up at the painting of Ernest Wheelright. His expression hadn't improved.

At the end of the room, the desk had been tipped forward. It was lying there, legs pointed toward the wall, like a turtle turned over on its back. The drawers had all been pulled out, emptied, and tossed into the corner, leaving a debris of stationery, pencils, and paper clips covering the floor. Next to the drawers was the overturned typewriter. Harold would probably have to do more than change the ribbon again to get it to type. The door to the inner office was open, so I carefully edged my way through the stuffing and went

CHAPTER THREE

in.

It looked like Yankee Stadium an hour after a game. The pictures had been ripped off the walls and left on the floor, some of the larger ones yanked out of the frames. The chairs and desk had all been overturned, and there was more office debris. Even the Venetian blind had been pulled down and dropped on the desk. In the middle of the floor was a small pile of pictures, neatly stacked. Next to it, on her knees, holding another picture with a smashed frame and shaking her head, was Winnie Adams in the same tired blue dress. She stopped and looked up at me.

"Don't get up," I said. "I can see you're having fun." It was a bad joke.

"Oh, Mr. Garrett." She stood up. Through her glasses, her eyes had the same misty look as the town through my windshield. "How could he? How could you?" She clenched her fists and thrust her arms straight down along her sides. "Your company will simply have to pay for this."

I looked around the room. "He didn't miss much, did he? Have the police been here?"

"The police? No. But that's a good idea." She was getting angry. "It's outrageous. He said that he was working with you and that he had to get something from the office. Then before I could even say anything, he came in here and did this. I just couldn't believe it. Then he went out there." She pointed toward the door, her breathing getting heavier. "My desk…the furniture…it's just terrible. How can you people do this?"

"Wait a minute." I righted two of the chairs. "Winnie, sit down." She did, hands folded in her lap. I pulled the other chair next to her and sat down. "Winnie, Frankie Bell isn't working with me. And I'm not with any insurance company. I'm a private investigator from Los Angeles. I was hired to find someone."

"Oh." She just looked at me now, blinking. Through her glasses, her magnified lashes looked a little like butterfly wings flapping.

"I'm afraid there's more." I reached out and held her wrist. "Charles…Mr. Stevens is dead."

She didn't say anything. She looked around the office, then turned back to me, tears beginning to show below the glasses. "I have to clean up the office.

Mr. Stevens will be angry."

She began to stand up, but I tightened my grip on her wrist. "No, Winnie. Listen to me. He's dead."

Then the tears started rolling. "What...what happened?"

I inhaled deeply and groped for the words. "He was shot. The police think he may have killed himself. I found him at Shady Lodge."

She looked stricken. "But he wasn't... He couldn't... Not there." She leaned over and buried her face in my sleeve; I could feel her sobs all the way down to my ankles. I just let it all run out.

After a while, she stopped and sat up, and pulled off her glasses. I handed her my handkerchief, and she started mopping her glasses instead of her face. She looked very different without the specs. Her eyes had an almond shape, the inner parts of the lids pointing toward the top of a pert nose. If you changed the pulled-back hair, plain dress, and baggy sweater, she wouldn't look half bad.

I leaned forward in the chair and put my hand on her arm as she looked up at me. "Winnie, there are some questions I have to ask."

"Yes?" She went on mopping.

"Do you have any idea what Bell was looking for?"

"No. He just came in here. I couldn't...." She looked down at the glasses, still mopping. "He's...I'm afraid of him."

"All right. Can you tell me about Mr. Stevens?"

She shivered a little, then squared her shoulders and sat up. "Tell you what?"

"About his business, his associates. Was he involved in any big deals recently?"

"No, not that I know of. This isn't a busy time at the foundry. He was just planning production for the spring and summer."

"What about his associates? Was he spending a lot of time with anyone in particular?"

"No, just the people in the plant, talking about tooling and repairs."

"Did you notice anything unusual recently, his manner, anything?"

"No," she said. "He was always very pleasant. He did miss work a few

CHAPTER THREE

times this month, and sometimes he'd come in late. But he remembered my birthday last week." She looked down. "He gave me flowers."

"How long have you had this job, Winnie?"

"About six months." She looked up again.

"How did you get it?"

"Through a mutual friend." She blinked and shifted her feet.

"Do you know Mrs. Stevens?"

The glasses went back on. "I met her a couple of times. She didn't come to the office much. She seems pleasant."

"Winnie…." I hesitated. "Could Mr. Stevens have been seeing someone, other than Mrs. Stevens?"

She bit her lip. "He was a good man. He wouldn't…he was a good man."

"Do you have any idea why he went to Shady Lodge?"

She stiffened. "That place, the stories I've heard. Why does anyone go there? Poor Mr. Stevens."

"Why does his death hit you so hard?"

She looked away and twisted my handkerchief in knots. "He was a wonderful man…to work for."

I leaned back in the chair and reached into my pocket, and pulled out a cigarette. "Yeah. He must have been. The police will probably want to question you, Winnie. But it won't hurt for you to take some time off. Would you like a ride home?"

"No!" It came out like a pistol shot. The whites of her eyes loomed behind her glasses, then instantly, she softened. "No, thank you. I'll just stay here and clean up." She looked around. "What a mess. Oh, dear. Will the police want to search the office too?"

"I don't think so. This was a professional job. They wouldn't find anything that Bell didn't."

"If that Mr. Bell comes back, should I call you?"

"There's nothing left to search. He won't be back. Are you sure you don't want me to take you home?"

"Yes, thank you." She got up and looked dejectedly out the window. "I'm sure."

I got up and walked out of the office, leaving her still holding my handkerchief. I paused at the door. Sure, he was a swell guy, wonderful to work for.

Chapter Four

I had some time to kill before noon, so I stopped at the same liquor store. The same old geezer was there, and I bought a bottle of the same Old Kentucky. It didn't take long for this town to become as familiar as an ex-wife. I drove out to Solomon's and parked about half a block away on the other side of the street.

I took a slug from the bottle, then put it back in the glove compartment and lit a cigarette. The smoke pummeled my lungs. I let it trail out slowly as I looked through the window. It was starting to rain, large drops, making a clunking sound on the hood of the car. Down the street, a little round old woman in a brown overcoat and tan kerchief was trudging up the steps of one of the rowhouses. She held a shopping bag that barely cleared the steps as she climbed. When she got to the top, she stopped and opened the door and, with both hands, dragged the bag in behind her and disappeared. She must have carried the weight of a lot of dreary winters.

I got tired of waiting, so I got out of the car and ducked through the rain until I reached the tailor shop. Solomon was speaking to a customer. He was a tall thin man with gray hair around the temples and a long, hooked nose. He wore a gray tweed overcoat and a plain gray hat with a black band.

"Next week, Thursday. You come by. I have the trousers."

"Make sure of the cuffs." The man had a deep resonant voice.

"The cuffs, I'll make sure. Next week."

The man turned, without even looking at me, and with long, careful steps, left the shop. Solomon looked at me.

"These people. They want everything tomorrow, just right."

I turned and watched the man march down the street, the drops of rain hopping above his hat. "Just make sure of the cuffs."

"Sure. It's a living, right?" He paused and rubbed his hands together. "So, Mr. Garrett, you're really wanting to see Frankie Bell? Maybe it's better you just leave him alone. He's trouble."

"That's why I'm here. But tell me about Manelli, the man you called Silver."

"Such a question." He sighed and shoved his hands into his pockets, and turned back toward the counter. He had on the same trousers and vest and white shirt. He might have slept in them.

"What can I tell?" he said. "He never comes here. I never see him. All I know are his measurements. Fine clothes he's got, expensive, nothing flashy like these kids. He must be older." He turned and looked at me with a wry curl to his upper lip. "But in good shape." He patted his stomach. "Not like me."

"What about Frankie Bell?"

"Him," he snorted. "Used to be a fighter. That man Silver was his manager, they say. One fight, Bell is getting beaten up pretty bad. But the other fighter is never fighting again. Nobody hears from him. Afterwards, Bell is staying here in Lancaster, and we all start paying."

"Has anybody seen Manelli?"

Before he could answer, we both caught sight of a Checker cab pulling up out front. Solomon turned to me with a grim set to his jaw.

"Okay, Mr. Solomon," I said. "I'll be in your back room. When Bell comes in, just act as if I'm not here."

"I should be lucky enough to be not here." He shuddered and rubbed his hands together.

I stepped into the back room behind the counter and stood beside the doorway, and waited. Bell came in with water dripping from his dark red hair and running off his leather jacket. I had never seen him standing up before. He must have been at least six-four, with shoulders almost as wide as his cab. He had one sleeve off, and he was using the jacket to protect a stack of suits hung over his arm. From the look of the fabric, I would need at least six months of steady cases to afford one.

CHAPTER FOUR

Bell laid the suits carefully out on the counter. Then he turned to Solomon. "Silver wants these tomorrow." I was surprised. He had a strangely high-pitched, raspy voice.

"Tomorrow!" Solomon was indignant. "Look. Am I an octopus? Have I got eight hands?" He pawed through the suits. "Maybe one suit tomorrow. But four suits, next Friday." I had to hand It to him. He stood up there with Bell, eyeball to belt buckle.

Bell took a handful of Solomon's vest and brought it up to the old man's chin. "If Silver says tomorrow, it's tomorrow. Understand?" He sounded like an alley cat cornering a rat. "Now where's my twenty?"

I stepped out through the doorway. "Do you get the twenty for shadowing somebody or just tearing up offices?"

Bell wheeled around, letting go of the vest. He hunched his shoulders and brought up two fists the size of hams. Solomon scurried around behind the counter.

"You're out of your weight class," I said, stepping around in front of those fists. I never was very bright.

Bell gave me a vacant look. Then his shoulders began to heave up and down, and he dropped his hands to his sides. His laughter came out, half whine, half cough. "Not now, flatfoot," he said after he got over his hysterics. "Later. Silver wants to see you."

"What a coincidence."

"Yeah." He laughed some more. "Now, let's go see Silver." Then he turned to Solomon. "I'll be here for the suits tomorrow."

I pressed my advantage. "I think Mr. Solomon said next Friday."

Bell glared at me, then started to laugh again and turned back to the old man. "Sure, Solomon. Next Friday."

I stepped closer. "You didn't hear me. It's *Mr.* Solomon."

Now Bell raised a cackle. "Yeah. *Mr.* Solomon."

"And no more twenties, right?"

The cackle was starting to peel the paint off the walls. "Sure. No more."

Solomon looked as if someone had just put ice in his shorts.

"Why don't I believe you, Bell? Do I have to start tailing you?"

"You're a card, Garrett." His laughter subsided. "C'mon. Silver's at the club. You got a car?"

"You should know."

He snickered. "Then you can follow me."

"That'll be a switch," I said. He laughed again. I was sorry I said it. He left and headed down the steps.

I turned back to Solomon and saw his worried expression. "It'll be all right," I said. It didn't reassure me either.

Outside, the rain was still coming down. I slogged over to the car, climbed in, and followed Bell down Central. After three blocks, he turned west onto Mayfair and went about six miles. It was secluded out there, large bare elm trees reaching over the road. Behind them were open fields and, every now and then, a farmhouse. And there were large square patches of uncovered earth that looked like gray scars on the landscape. Before they could heal, the farmers would be at them again.

After another mile, there were more trees, and Bell turned behind one of them. I followed him up a winding driveway and over a rise to the front of the club. It was a two-story mansion painted gray with white trim, and on top of the flat tiled roof, a tall red brick chimney was showing a curl of smoke. The few windows all had Venetian blinds, no shutters, and all were closed. The walkway leading up to the front door was covered with a green carpet, and over the carpet was a green awning stretching up over a handful of steps. The driveway swung by the end of the carpet, then wound around to the back of the house. At the end of the awning, an attendant wearing a trench coat and navy pin-striped trousers was standing there watching me. I stopped the car, and he came around and opened up the door on my side.

"I'll park it for you, sir," he said. I got out, and he handed me a ticket. It was the size of one of my business cards, but it had a glossy silver-colored finish.

I ducked under the awning and headed up the walkway. Bell was already standing on the steps, smiling. As I walked up the steps, I looked past him to a pair of dark wooden double doors, highly polished with plain wooden handles. Mounted just to the left, a little below eye level, was a small silver plaque. It read SILVER CLUB.

CHAPTER FOUR

Bell yanked one of the doors open and growled, "This way." We went into a dark, narrow passage, through two more doors, and into a small lobby. It was covered in a rich green carpet, and the walls were painted a soft beige. There were open doorways on both sides, appearing to lead to the main room behind. Between the doors was a tall wooden captain's desk, with a pinched-faced man with thick black hair and bushy eyebrows that made a shelf over the bridge of his nose standing behind it, wearing a tux. Bell went over and mumbled something to him. Suddenly, the eyebrows popped up. "Oh yes," the man said and motioned to me. "Right this way."

I followed him through the door to the right into the club, with Bell just behind. The room was long, with no windows and a hardwood floor polished like a bowling alley. The walls were painted the same beige as the lobby, and about every ten feet were placed silver light fixtures. Each one had three thin stems curling up, holding mock candles with tapered electric bulbs, the kind with the filaments showing. A chandelier sparkled overhead, with the same thin stems and the same tapered bulbs. There must have been fifty tables, with white linen tablecloths, napkins folded at each place, and freshly polished silverware. It could have taken the rest of the day to walk around the room.

At the far end along the wall was a square stage surrounded by a semicircular area cleared for dancing. Each corner of the stage held a silver champagne bucket filled with yellow roses. And between the buckets in the middle of the stage was an upright piano with a single silver candlestick on top. Crouched over the keyboard, a gray-haired Negro in a tux was playing soft jazz and slowly bobbing his head up and down.

There was a pair of swinging doors in the corner to the right. As I watched, a busboy in a white dinner jacket came out carrying a silver tray the size of a manhole cover. On the far side, opposite the kitchen, was a single unmarked door. It didn't look like the way out. The place was about a third filled, mostly men in dark suits. Some of them were eating, but most were huddled over the tables talking, occasionally glancing around at the other tables.

As I stepped through the door, a young brunette came over. She had on a white collar, a black bow tie, a formal black coat with tails and no sleeves,

THE SILVER SETUP

and above the waist, not much else. Below was a pair of skintight black shorts that would boost anybody's blood pressure, black net stockings, and heels you could hammer through a two-by-four. She took my coat and hat, frowned at my suit, and went into the lobby.

The pinched-faced man led me to a table next to the wall, then retreated. Bell pointed one of his hams at the table. "Wait here, Garrett. I'll go tell Silver you're here." He turned and waded through the tables to the far corner and went through the single door. I sat down and tried not to wrinkle the tablecloth.

Just when I was starting to feel self-conscious about my suit, a tall set of curves came over to my table, wearing the same kind of outfit as the brunette. This one was a blonde, with dancing green eyes and a body you couldn't forget.

"I'm Daphne," she said. "And you must be Mr. Garrett."

"I guess that's no secret."

"What would you like, handsome? They said you've got a free ticket."

"In that case, tell me about Gloria."

The eyes stopped dancing. "I mean, what do you want to order?"

"I didn't come here for lunch. Do you know Gloria Tempest?"

She leaned over, holding a pad and pencil as if she were writing my order. "I hardly know her. She sings here and helps cover the tables. Or at least she used to. She hasn't been here in a week. Nobody's seen her."

"Did she spend time with anybody?"

She looked as if I had just stepped on her foot. "Look. I like Gloria. We're not close, but we get along."

"Then help her out. Talk to me."

"Nobody's supposed to know," she whispered, "because he's married. And because... Well, he's important."

"How important?"

She straightened up and looked over her shoulder, then she looked back. "Mr. Garrett, please just give me your order."

"Sure, Daphne." I leaned back in the chair. "Bring me a Scotch."

Her eyes brightened again. "Any particular brand?"

42

CHAPTER FOUR

"No, just pick an expensive one. Put it on the table, and I'll watch the ice melt."

She floated away, and I couldn't help watching the tails on her jacket whisk along the edges of the tables. She disappeared into the kitchen, and I looked around the room. About three tables away, under the chandelier, four men in black suits were leaning elbow to elbow, puffing on cigars and mumbling. One of them was fat and bald, with a leering mouth and jowls that chewed nonchalantly on his cigar. He turned and slowly gave me the once-over.

The blonde returned with my Scotch and no desire to talk. So, I sipped a little and listened to the piano player do a sleepy version of "As Time Goes By." It was like a scene out of a Humphrey Bogart movie. I had just finished about half the drink when Bell burst through the door in the far corner. A couple of strides and he was standing next to my table.

"All right, Garrett," he said. "Silver says to bring you up."

A long gulp finished the Scotch, and I felt it burn its way down as I followed Bell across the room. We went through the door, and he led the way up the stairs. They were covered in a plush green carpet that seemed to wrap itself around my feet. At the top, I saw a door with a small nameplate that said simply, SILVER. Bell knocked, and we went inside.

The office was small and dark, with no windows and the same green carpet. The dark paneled walls were bare, except for two silver light fixtures, tastefully plain. Three brown leather chairs formed a semicircle facing a desk that filled half the room. Along the wall to the left was a small serving table that held a polished silver tea set. And behind the desk, a wall shelf held two more champagne buckets with yellow roses, like the ones downstairs. The room was lit only by a desk lamp that created a bright spot in the middle of the desk. It also showed a man leaning over the desk, writing.

Bell moved toward the desk. "I got Garrett, boss."

The man said, "Sit," while he kept on writing. He might have been talking to a cocker spaniel. Bell pointed me to a chair, then moved over next to the serving table and leaned against the wall, arms folded, as I peered across the desk at Manelli. It was hard to tell while he sat, but I guessed that he was about my height and maybe fifteen pounds heavier. He wore a pearl-gray suit and vest, with a white shirt and matching gray tie. His shirt cuffs were fastened by thick round links that looked like silver hockey pucks, and a round silver tie pin showed above his vest.

He had a rounded, swarthy face with a wide thick-lipped mouth and receding chin. A wide nose with flared nostrils appeared flattened against his face, seeming to puff out his pockmarked cheeks. His breath came out heavily, almost forced, sounding like a bellows in a fireplace; his eyes were shadowed by thick white eyebrows, the left one shortened by a scar that extended from his forehead down across his temple. Over it all, like whitecaps on an ocean, were waves of thick white hair glistening under the desk lamp. He looked about fifty.

I lit a cigarette and tossed the match into a silver tray on the front of the desk. Finally, Manelli put down his pen and reached over and flipped a wall switch, brightening the fixtures along the sides. Then he folded both hands and eyed me across the desk. He wore a look of detached curiosity, as If he'd just seen something stirring in his wastebasket.

I looked around the room at all the glitter, then looked back and nodded toward Manelli. "You must have had Paul Revere for your decorator."

Chapter Five

Manelli leaned back in his chair, his white hair shining. "You're a smart guy, ain't ya, Garrett? I heard about you at Joe Hinson's trial. Big California gumshoe. Tough guy. Come to town to cause trouble."

"It's no trouble putting the slam on weasels like Floren and the Hinson boys."

He poked his nose with a meaty finger, his cufflink catching my eye. "Too bad about Mannie. He mighta worked out."

"Yeah, too bad. I've been crying all week."

He put his hands in his lap and shrugged out a couple of heavy wheezing sounds. I think he was laughing. "A real smart guy, real funny."

Then Manelli sat up, his eyebrows straining into a scowl, and he hissed at me out of the side of his mouth. "But you're right about the Hinsons. That punk Joe. All he cared about was biting off territory, not remembering friends. Friends are important. You take care of friends. You don't try to chisel 'em. You got friends, ain't ya, Garrett?"

"Sure. Frankie and I have gotten to be real pals." I nodded toward Bell. He just shifted his feet and looked bored.

Manelli snorted. "That Joe and his broads, not keeping his mind on business. And his brother Arnie, another punk. Getting messed up with that young California chick. They both deserved what they got."

I felt my stomach tighten. "And you saw that they got it."

His expression eased, and the right side of his mouth began to curl up. "We all do what we can. How about you, Garrett? What do you do?"

"Me? Oh, I just pound the pavement, ducking expensive hoods and looking up dead husbands for rich widows."

He sat back and folded his hands across his chest. "That's supposed to mean something?"

"Hell, no. Why should it? This Isn't your town, your state. You don't own the politicians and the businessmen. You're not into the pockets of every little guy trying to make a buck. You're clean. You wouldn't know about Charles Stevens meeting with a chunk of lead in a crummy motel that you don't own. All you do is sit here in your club and send your trained ape out to run errands."

Bell made a move at me, but Manelli put his hand down on the desk and gave him a look that would turn a sizzling August morning to sleet. Bell went back to the wall, and Manelli turned to me. "So, what's it to you?"

"Just an unhappy client with a dead husband who might have been wrapped up with somebody from your club. But you wouldn't know about that."

"Maybe I do, maybe I don't." He dug at his nose again. "Maybe I got friends who keep an eye out, who tell me things. Stevens was a big man in this town. Maybe he was getting too big, forgetting his friends."

"What friends did he have at Shady Lodge?"

He leaned back and gave me a smug look. "It's a nice friendly place."

"Sure, it is. What was Stevens to you?"

His features turned slowly bland, and he let out a bored-sounding sigh. "Stop reaching, Garrett. You won't get anything."

"Fine." I crushed out my cigarette. "So why am I here? You didn't send your goon after me just so you could admire my clothes."

He reached into a desk drawer to his right and pulled out some foreign-looking cigarettes in a silver box wrapped in cellophane. As he began to open the box, Bell reached into his pocket, pulled out a lighter, and in one motion, flicked it on and held It out over the desk. Manelli peeled a piece of pale blue wrapper off the cigarettes on the inside of the box, took one out, and lit it. Then he rolled the wrapper into a tight little ball and dropped it into the ashtray. Bell moved back again, and Manelli blew a rancid cloud in my direction. "Maybe I want to hire you."

CHAPTER FIVE

"With all your friends? What could I do for you?"

"Find somebody, a girl from the club. About a week ago, she took some money and went on the lam. You find her and bring her back."

"What's her name?"

"Gloria. Gloria Tempest. She worked downstairs, waiting tables and singing. Pretty good pipes too. Anyway, about a week ago, she dips into the till down there after closing and just takes a powder."

"Why don't you go to the police?" I was just full of good questions.

"We don't want the police. We just want to keep this between friends. You can understand that, can't ya, Garrett?" He looked like a hungry man getting ready to carve a roast.

"How much did she take?"

He shrugged, and his hands fell in his lap again. "Doesn't matter. Friends don't do what she did. And I want her back." He reached into the desk and then handed me a picture of a slender blonde with a long sweep of hair crossing her forehead and falling over her right shoulder. "That's her."

I nodded. "Tough losing a friend like this."

"Yeah, she's a looker, all right." He scribbled something on the top page of his desk calendar, tore it off, and handed it to me. It read *712 Steiner St., Apt 4*. It had two curled corners. "That's her address."

I lit another cigarette. "So, it was right there on the tip of your tongue. You didn't even have to look it up."

"I know all about my friends."

"You and Gloria must have been *very* friendly."

He grinned, showing a wide set of jagged yellow teeth. "Like I said, friends are important."

"You must have had my friend Frankie check her place, so she couldn't be there."

He just kept grinning.

"Did she have any other friends? Some way I can get a line on her?"

He shrugged. "Some of the girls downstairs."

"You must have asked them. They haven't seen her?"

"I told ya. She skipped a week ago."

"She's not here, and she's not at home. So, how do I find her? She could be anywhere."

His grin got even wider. "You're the big-city detective. You figure it out."

I threw my best shot. "Was she seeing Charles Stevens?"

The teeth disappeared, and you could almost see the icicles form on the edge of the desk. "Maybe she was, maybe she wasn't. Maybe she killed him. Maybe you don't hear so good. Anyway, I want her back."

"And maybe I'm not interested in working for a creep like you."

He put his elbows on the desk. "I checked. You get thirty a day plus expenses. I'll double it."

"Do you buy all your friends that way?"

He snarled at me. "You ain't so smart, Garrett."

"You're right. I'm dumb." I picked up the blue ball of paper in his ashtray and let it drop. "Just dumb enough to know that you were in the room where Stevens was killed. Maybe you and he weren't such good friends."

"You don't know nothin'." He bit off his words like a butcher slicing salami. "Maybe you'll find this town ain't such a friendly place. Maybe people here don't like a smart-mouthed dick coming in from out of town to put the arm on somebody."

"Aw, stop it. You're terrifying me."

"I mean it, Garrett," he snapped. "There are ways of taking care of a troublemaker. Maybe this ain't L.A., but there's still enough heat. If you don't want to be a friend, then maybe it's healthier for you in California."

"And maybe I'll try to find Gloria Tempest. But you don't have to double my fee. Just tell my friend here to lay off the little man in the tailor shop and stop following me."

Manelli looked over at Bell, then turned back to me. He stared at me for a minute, then be started to grin. He seemed relieved. "Okay. But don't forget your friends, Garrett."

I stood up and headed for the door. When I reached it, I stopped and looked back. "Sure, friend. Maybe."

I left the club as quickly as I could and headed down the drive, and cruised back toward town. It was still raining, but I hardly noticed. When I reached

CHAPTER FIVE

Central, I parked in front of a drugstore and reached for my friend, Old Kentucky. It burned into my gullet, drawing my mind off the smell of Manelli's cigarette. And I just sat there.

After a while, I began to feel the cold, so I went into the drugstore and called the hotel. No message from Ed Rawls. It was too early to check in on Lenore Stevens, so I headed back to Shady Lodge.

The rain was slowing as I arrived. There were no cars, and the cabins were all dark. The curtains were drawn in the main house, but there was a light on downstairs. I shivered a little as I got out of the car. I wasn't sure it was from the weather. On the porch, I stopped and looked back for a minute at the empty driveway and the road beyond. In the early afternoon drizzle, the place showed all the charm of a cemetery. Still, I went in.

Ralph was behind the desk doing a crossword puzzle. As soon as he saw me, he jumped up and edged toward the rear doorway behind the desk. His mustache was twitching, and the smirk was gone.

"Hey, look, Garrett, I don't want trouble."

"Sure," I said. "You're just an all-American kid minding his own business in a nice clean place. Why should I care if you put the finger on me for a couple of strong-arm cops?"

"I hadda do that." He edged closer to the door. "Moran. He comes here a lot. I had to tell him about you."

"Relax, kid. I'm not here to muscle you. But I want the straight goods. How long was Stevens coming here?"

His mustache settled down, and he loosened his tie. Then he moved tentatively forward and put both hands on the desk. "About six months. He was a regular."

"Did he see anyone besides Gloria Tempest?"

"No, just her. At first, he came only a couple of times a month, but lately it was every week, every Tuesday."

"But yesterday was Thursday. Why did he come in then?"

"I don't know." He looked genuinely curious. "He just came in and paid his bill, like always."

"How did he pay?"

"By check. All our customers pay the motel, and we settle up with the girls. That way there's nothing to trace. Like I said, Stevens was a regular. He paid once a month."

"What a service to the community." I leaned against the desk, and he backed away a little. "Did you hear the shot?"

"Down there at the end? Listen, you can't hear anything that goes on in those cabins. Our customers like it that way."

"And they don't like to be seen either, huh?" He just stared at me. I walked around behind the desk and stood next to him, close enough so I could count the whiskers in his mustache. "Are you sure you didn't see anyone else go in or out of Number Seven?"

"No."

I could see droplets of sweat starting to form just over his eyebrows and along his temples.

"There was nobody, in or out. But look, I don't watch. I just stay in here and mind my own business. I don't want trouble."

"So, someone else could have been here?"

He brought up his hand, loosening his tie even more. His fingers were trembling.

"Take it easy," I said and reached into my pocket and laid out a five on the desk. "What about it?"

Ralph looked down at the bill and licked his lips. Then he looked up at me. "All right. I didn't see her around the cabin. She was in the lot. I saw her get into a car and leave."

"Who?"

His eyes turned glassy, and he ducked his head. Then he muttered half to himself, as if he were cursing something in the dark. "Gloria."

"What time was she here?"

"About three, I guess."

"Are you sure it was Gloria?"

"It was her. I mean, I didn't exactly see her face, but that…it was her."

"You know her that well?"

"She was always nice to me, treated me like I was more than just a flunky."

CHAPTER FIVE

His teeth clenched. "I hated it that she worked down there in that cabin. I really hated it."

"Enough to kill the man who was down there paying for her?"

He stopped and gazed at me with a look of bewilderment. "No."

"All right, Ralph," I said. Then as he exhaled deeply and reached down for the bill. I caught his wrist. "What about Silver?"

The blood left his face like water draining from a sink. "Please, Mr. Garrett. I shouldn't even be talking to you."

"He was there, wasn't he?"

"I didn't see him, just his car."

"When?"

"Later, about five, a little before you came."

"And that's all?"

"Yeah, that's all. Honest."

I picked up the bill, folded it, and stuffed it in his pocket. "Okay, Ralph. Thanks." I turned and headed for the door, but before I could reach it, he spoke again.

"Mr. Garrett, about Gloria. I don't care what she does here. She's not like that, not really. She wouldn't hurt anybody. If somebody killed Stevens, it wasn't Gloria." From his look, he was talking to himself as much as to me.

"Maybe not, Ralph." I turned and left.

On the way to the Stevens's house, I swung by the hotel. There was still no message from Rawls, so I bought a paper and sat down with it in the lobby. By now, Charles Stevens was all over the front page.

LANCASTER MOURNS LOCAL BUSINESSMAN

> Prominent Lancaster business leader Charles Stevens was found dead in a local motel late Thursday. According to police, Stevens died from a single gunshot wound to the chest, probably self-inflicted. Funeral services are scheduled for early Saturday morning.

The rest was just background on Stevens and the foundry. The biggest man in town got the smallest obituary. There was nothing about Shady Lodge or the ransacked office. Whatever Wells was thinking, he was keeping it to himself.

I quickly browsed through the rest of the paper and was about to toss it away when my eye caught on an ad in the personals. "C, I have it. See you same place. G." Probably coincidence. I put in a call to the paper, asked for Classified, and then heard a sweet young voice on the other end. I gave her some fast talk, and finally, she told me that the ad had been placed three days ago to run until the end of the week. But the ad was paid for in cash, and there was no record of who placed it. I asked if she remembered a long-haired blonde. She didn't. She said she was the only blonde there and offered to prove it.

I didn't feel much like fun and games, so I went out and got into the DeSoto. By the time I got to the Stevens's house, the rain had stopped. The sun was dipping over a row of trees past the house to the left. And it was getting colder. I got out of the car and turned up my coat collar against an icy wind that seemed to know where I would feel it the most. As I headed for the brick steps, I noticed a dusty blue Ford parked in front of the house, the kind a cop would drive. Before I could reach the front door, it opened, and there was Rogers. "Mr. Garrett, you're expected." He stepped aside and held the door open.

I stepped inside. "Thanks, Rogers. How's Mrs. Stevens holding up?"

"Rather well, sir, I should say. They're waiting for you now."

"They?"

"Yes, sir. Mrs. Stevens and Lieutenant Wells, in the drawing room."

He took my coat and hat and sauntered off. I went across the hall to the drawing room and found Lenore Stevens talking to Wells. "…that's why I hired him. He's here to help."

As I walked through the door, they both gaped in my direction. Then Wells moved around the sofa and came toward me, the furrows in his brow jutting forward like truck bumpers.

"Garrett, I thought we understood each other. You were supposed to be

CHAPTER FIVE

on your way out of town."

"It was on my mind until I ran into a lug named Frankie Bell. Besides, this town kind of grows on you."

"What do you know about Frankie Bell?" His expression became even more grim.

"I know that he's been following me in his cab, and that he spends his spare time shaking down the local merchants."

"That's not news," he grumbled. "We know about his racket. We just can't get anybody to testify. But that's no reason for you to stick around."

"Maybe not. But there's a tailor named Solomon you should talk to. And if it matters to you, I also know that Frankie Bell was at Shady Lodge the night Charles Stevens died." I looked over at Lenore Stevens. The muscles in her jaw were set tight. I suddenly wished I had waited before unloading on Wells.

He stood back, hands on hips, his brow knitted in uncertainty. "How do you know he was there?"

"I saw him, or at least his cab. He'd been tailing me since I first got into town. I spotted his cab at the motel while I was waiting for your boys to show up. I chased him a couple of miles, but I lost him on the highway."

Now Wells turned surly, and he started pointing a finger toward my chest. "Look, Garrett. This is an official police investigation. Get it? I don't want you tramping around town on your own, getting into scrapes with Bell." He hesitated. "Or anyone else."

"Like Silver?"

"Damn it, Garrett. You're out of your territory. Go back to Los Angeles."

"Sorry, Lieutenant. Not while I have a paying client."

He turned back to Lenore Stevens. "Is that right? Do you still insist on keeping him here?"

She sounded a little uncertain, but she came through. "Well, Mr. Garrett and I have some unfinished business."

"What business?" He was starting to sound like a prosecutor.

She inhaled deeply, straightened, and stretched her shoulders back. Her voice was more firm. "Family business, Lieutenant. I'm sure you understand."

THE SILVER SETUP

He turned back to me, his forehead set at full scowl. "I think I'm beginning to. Remember what I said, Garrett. Stay out of my way and go on home. Don't cross the line." He excused himself and made a curt exit.

Lenore Stevens stared at the door for a long moment. Then she turned to me with a look of surprise. "What do you suppose he meant about beginning to understand?"

"Nothing. He's just a frustrated cop."

"Would you like a drink?" She motioned to the same decanter of brandy on the coffee table. I helped myself.

She walked slowly over to the fireplace, put her hand on the mantel, and stared down for a time. She looked drawn and pale. "Maybe Lieutenant Wells is right," she said quietly. "Maybe you should leave."

"It's too late for that. I know too much."

"You do?" She looked at me with very round eyes in a childlike face.

"That's right. I know that your husband had at least one visitor in his motel room, maybe more. I know that a flashy hood named Manelli threatened me and tried to hire me and seems to be afraid of something. I know that an ape named Bell tailed me around town, showed up at Shady Lodge, and then tore your husband's office apart searching it. And I know that some heavy-handed cops roughed me up, then suggested I leave town. But they haven't exactly run me out, probably because they don't believe the suicide angle either. A lot of people seem to be interested in what I might find out about your husband. Aren't you?"

She sighed and dropped her hand to her side, and her eyes hardened like quick-drying cement. "Yes, of course. I'm sorry, Mr. Garrett. It's just that so much has happened so quickly."

"What can you tell me about your husband's business?"

She folded her hands in front of her and stepped away from the fireplace. "I don't know very much, really. It's very complicated, I know that. It was investments mostly, other companies, real estate. Of course, he spent most of his time at the foundry."

"You said he was under a lot of pressure lately. I talked with his secretary. He wasn't under any strain at Wheelright. What else could have been

CHAPTER FIVE

bothering him?"

She rubbed her hands together. "Politics perhaps. Several of his friends were encouraging him to run for the Senate. I think he may have decided to do it." She paused. "Still, he did talk about getting out."

"Was Manelli one of his friends?"

"Oh, no." She became wide-eyed. "He couldn't have been. Mr. Garrett, are you sure that Charles was murdered? Could that man...?"

I nodded. "He could. He's afraid of something. And he's looking for something he thinks your husband had. That's why he wanted to hire me. He thinks I might find it." I watched her carefully as she digested what I said. I wasn't sure how much she could take, or how much I could. "Mrs. Stevens, if you haven't heard it yet, you will soon. Your husband was meeting regularly with a girl named Gloria Tempest at Shady Lodge."

She looked down at the floor, then walked slowly over to the bookcase by the window. She stared out the window for what seemed like a week. Then just as I was trying to unglue my feet from the floor, she turned and gave it to me like a Bob Feller fastball.

"Mr. Garrett, there's no point denying it. Charles and I didn't have much of a marriage. I appreciate your trying to spare my feelings. Naturally, I'm saddened by his death, and I'm shocked over the way it may have happened. But I don't miss Charles, or his drinking, or his...affairs. Yes, I've suspected for some time. I guess I just didn't want to face the truth. If I sound bitter, it's not about Charles."

She walked back over to the coffee table and poured some more brandy. Then she looked at me with matter-of-fact eyes. "My parents weren't wealthy. They sacrificed a lot to buy me good clothes, send me to good schools. They wanted me to have more than they did. They were delighted when I married Charles. And so was I. But before long, I think we both realized the marriage was a mistake. Still, we carried on for the sake of appearances. It was difficult living with Charles, a man who came by everything naturally, who controlled everything. If only he had had more room for me. But I guess I didn't give him what he needed either. I...I couldn't have children."

"That happens with a lot of people. You don't have to think of it as a tragedy." I put my glass down on the coffee table. "I didn't mean to upset you."

"You didn't." She paused and put her glass down too. "Mr. Garrett, about last night. I'm so embarrassed. I'm afraid I didn't behave very well."

"You did okay. You handled it as well as anyone hearing that her husband had just died."

She moved over and stood next to me. "You're very understanding." Then she put her hand on my arm. "I can see why Edward has such respect for you."

I felt my collar starting to tighten, and I realized how warm the room was getting. "I have to check back at my hotel. I'm expecting a call from him."

"Of course." She kept her hand on my arm. "The funeral is tomorrow. Will you come?"

"No. You're not paying me to go to funerals. I'll see you later." I started to leave. "By the way, did you go out last night?"

She dropped her hand, and her eyelids fluttered a little. "Why, yes, I had dinner with some friends at the country club." She cocked her head to one side. "Is that important?"

"Probably not. It's just a habit of mine to ask questions." I turned and walked out.

All the way back to the hotel, I felt uneasy. It was dark, and the wind had picked up, as if winter wanted to get in its last licks. As I pulled up in front of the hotel, I reached into my pocket for a cigarette and felt the paper Manelli had given me with Gloria Tempest's address. I hesitated for a minute, then went inside. The old lady handed me a message: *"Phone Rawls, Los Angeles."*

It wasn't that late, and I thought about going out again. But then I remembered the bottle of Old Kentucky waiting in my room, so I made a beeline upstairs. As I walked up the hall, I heard Glenn Miller's orchestra on somebody's radio, and across the hall from my room, I caught the sounds of a couple yelling and going at each other like Dempsey and Tunney. I slid my key into the lock, opened the door, and stopped. The dark was interrupted by red neon spasms from the cafeteria across the street. And there was a faint smell of jasmine. Then the voice.

CHAPTER FIVE

"Don't turn on the light."

Chapter Six

I eased into the room and quietly pulled the door shut behind me. While my eyes took their time adjusting to the dark, I thought about the Luger in my bag and just shook my head. I could almost make out the room. In the occasional glare from the cafeteria, it looked about the way I remembered—seedy. But there was a shadowed figure sitting in the corner, and a rustle of movement.

"I have to talk to you." It was a soft voice, feminine, but deep and husky with a hardness underneath, like reinforced concrete. "I didn't want anyone to know."

Suddenly I didn't care about the Luger. "Well, I'm not just anyone, so you're safe." I crossed the room to the window and started to pull down the shade.

"What are you doing?"

I reached over and switched on the small lamp on the nightstand. "What I always do in the dark."

She recoiled like a pickpocket with burnt fingers and brought both fists up under her chin. "Don't do that!"

"Relax. If anyone's watching, they'd think it was funny if I came in here and didn't turn on the light."

She eased a little and brought her fists down to her lap, but they were still fists. There was a wire hanger resting on a nail on the back of the door, so I hung up my coat. Then I took off my hat and laid it on the edge of the bed, and sat down next to it, facing her.

"Mr. Garrett?"

I didn't answer. She already knew it was my room.

CHAPTER SIX

"I'm Gloria Tempest."

She looked down and folded her hands together into one large tight fist. I sat there and watched her. There wasn't much to see, just a tan trench coat buttoned up around her with the collar raised, and on her feet a pair of black open-toed shoes. They were the kind that might just get her from her front door to the curb, so she could climb into her limousine. Between the coat and the shoes was a matched set of trim ankles and calves that looked as if they would cost a lot.

I couldn't see much of her face. She was wearing a round blue-gray hat with a broad-sloping brim turned down over her forehead. It almost hid the blond hair done up underneath. Almost. There was still enough showing to catch the light from the lamp; it had a carefully brushed silvery look, something like fresh cornsilk. But except for the end of a narrow nose and smooth, rounded chin, her face was hidden. She sat there now, squeezing a small shiny black clutch purse in her lap, squeezing it the way you might go after the last bit of toothpaste in an old, wrinkled tube. It was the movement of someone very nervous or very frightened or both.

Finally, she spoke. "I...I need your help."

"Get in line."

"You were at the lodge. I saw you. You know about...about Charles."

I nodded.

"I saw the police there. And I saw...." She squeezed the purse some more. "I'm so scared."

"Me too, sister. What scares you?"

She glanced up at me and then quickly put her head down again. She swallowed hard. "I saw Silver. Outside the cabin. He killed Charles, and now he's after me."

"Why would Manelli kill Stevens?"

She fidgeted nervously. "I...I'm not sure. Charles and I were...." She left it hanging and turned her head toward the window. "I just don't know what to do."

"I'd say you've already done plenty."

"What?" She looked up, but her face was still shadowed by the brim of her hat.

"You heist some dough from your boss and make tracks. Then the man you've been entertaining for six months at the motel turns up dead. So, I get to break the news to his widow; the cops beat me up; Manelli threatens me, and now you want me to help you. Lady, I'm the one who needs help."

She looked down again. "It's not the way you think."

"Why would I think anything? So what if you took some money from your boyfriend's club? He's just a cheap hood. And milking a bored businessman? If you hadn't, another neat little trick would have."

"You don't understand."

"You're probably right. I never did understand murder. Your friend Silver thinks maybe you killed Stevens. But that wouldn't make sense, would it? You must have been really sad, seeing your bankroll permanently ventilated."

She jumped up and glared at me from under her hat brim and waved the purse in my face. Her voice was even deeper, and it hissed out at me through her teeth, almost in a whisper. "Don't you talk to me that way. Who are you? A gumshoe. A leech, living off people in trouble."

I stood up in front of her. "They're already in trouble when they come to me. And knock off the righteous indignation. In your circle, it just doesn't fit."

She aimed the purse for the side of my head, but I caught her wrist in mid-swing. "If you meant that for yourself," I said, "your aim is bad."

"I hate you. I hate the way you talk. You think you can judge a person." She wrenched her arm out of my grasp. Her jasmine scent danced through my nostrils, and I started to forget that she might be a killer. Then she sneered and hissed at me.

"You're so *nice*."

"I'm not in a nice business."

She put both hands on her purse and let her arms fall in front of her. "I guess you're just like all the rest of them. I talked to Ralph. He said I should see you. He said that you were smart, that you might help me. I guess he was wrong."

"Only about my being smart." I could see her eyes now. They were big and

CHAPTER SIX

round and very blue with flecks of light. But they didn't look as good as they should have. They were red and swollen, and they had a drained look.

"Sit down," I said and eased her back toward the chair. "Want a drink?"

"Please." It didn't sound bitter, just tired.

I went into the bathroom and rinsed out two glasses. When I came back into the room, she was pulling off her coat. I opened the drawer of the nightstand and took out the elixir for all occasions. Then I poured a good slug of Old Kentucky into each glass and handed one to her.

"There's no ice," I said, "and I don't think you want me calling room service."

"This is okay, thank you." She took a deep swallow and didn't flinch.

I watched her as she took off her hat and rested it on the arm of the chair over her coat. She was wearing a plain, high-necked black dress with long sleeves and a slit up the side. It fitted her like a second skin. And there was no concealing that body; you could see it in sculpture in almost any museum.

Her blond hair cascaded over her shoulders in gentle waves, with just a hint of curl at the ends. It framed a face with high cheekbones, showing a pleasant flush, a graceful chin, a straight slender nose, and two of the bluest eyes I'd ever seen. She had very red full lips, and she had the lower one sucked in under her teeth as she studied what was left in her glass. She didn't study it long. She finished it quickly and held it out toward me. "Could I have another?"

I poured some more into her glass, sat down on the bed, and watched her, while she watched me. We watched each other. Then I guess she got tired of it.

"You're very hard, aren't you?"

I nodded. "So are you."

"They made me that way. He did. But it's not like you think."

"We've been through what I think. Just tell it."

She took another swallow. "I didn't steal any of Silver's money. I only took what was mine, what he owed me. He was refusing to pay me for my work at the club. So, I just took what I was due and left."

"And here I thought your work was a labor of love."

"Very funny. I worked hard at the club. I needed the money." She looked down toward her purse, and her voice softened. "The pay was good. But it's not easy dealing with all those men, those…."

"Yeah, I saw some of them. If it's your money, why is Manelli so anxious to get it back?"

"He's not. He's angry at me about…about Charles."

"Wanted you for himself, huh? Private stock?"

"It's not like that," she flashed. "I never slept with him. I never would. Not with any of them. At least not there, and not unless they paid for it."

I didn't say anything.

She rubbed her hands together, almost as if she were washing them, and I could see moisture starting to form across her lower lids.

"I always felt so cheap, so small," she said. "But they didn't care. They're all pigs. The things they'd do or want me to do. To them, I was just meat."

She rested her hands on the arms of the chair and leaned back, a look of tired resignation on her face. She couldn't have been much past thirty, but at that moment, she looked It.

"Maybe you're right," she said. "Silver always hangs on to what's his. What he doesn't have, he wants even more. And he'll do anything to get it. Nobody gets in his way, nobody. Maybe I'm just fooling myself. I'll never get away. Not now."

"You mean with Stevens dead?"

She nodded, and a tear trickled down toward her chin.

"But why the flesh-peddling? I heard that you sing."

"Silver owns my contract. He took it over when I was singing in Philadelphia. He brought me here and wouldn't ever let me work anywhere else. I needed money, a lot of money, for personal reasons. So, I started working a cabin at Shady Lodge. Men would see me at the club and then come out to the motel, so they could brag about it to their friends. I got top dollar." Now the bitterness was beginning to show. "Silver was mad at first. But then he got the idea he could use me that way, for his business. I hated doing it, but I had no choice. Then I met Charles."

"Look," I said. "You're getting ahead of me."

I poured us both some more Old Kentucky and drank it down while she

CHAPTER SIX

caught her breath. Then I lit a cigarette, sat down on the bed again, and looked at her.

"Go back to Philadelphia," I said.

She lifted her glass and took just a sip this time. I could almost see her memory tracing back behind her eyes. She inhaled deeply, composing her thoughts, and softly cleared her throat.

"I grew up in Philadelphia. My mother died when I was very young, and my father drank himself to death when I was still in high school. That left me and my kid sister. We lived with an aunt until I was old enough to move out and take my sister with me. I quit school so I could go to work." There was just the hint of a mocking smile. "Even then, I could have done what I do now. I had offers. But I took a job as a waitress. Only that wasn't enough."

She folded her hands in her lap and stared down at them. "My sister was ill. They said she had tuberculosis and that she needed treatment. I couldn't afford to send her to a sanitarium. The doctors agreed to let her stay with me, but she needed regular treatments and medicine. It was expensive."

She looked up at me now. "I had a friend from high school, Ellie Petrone. Her father owned a big nightclub. They said he was in the rackets, but I didn't care." Her eyes brightened a little. "He gave me a job. He paid me well, and he let me sing to earn extra money. I did all right. My sister got better, and I started to think I might even have a career. Then Silver took over." The brightness faded, and her jaw began to tighten. "He worked for Mr. Petrone at first. I don't know what he did, but everybody was afraid of him. He and Mr. Petrone used to argue, about how to run the club and other things, I guess. Then one morning, outside the club, they found Mr. Petrone in his car. He'd been strangled." She brought up her hand and chewed on a knuckle. "There was a wire around his neck." She shuddered. "He'd been garroted. And I never saw Ellie again." She stopped and looked at me, and finally, she broke. There was no sound, just tears.

I waited. After a while, she reached into her purse for a handkerchief.

"Yeah," I said. "That's the way the mob does it. So Manelli took over. Then, later on, it got too hot for him there, and he moved out here to Lancaster."

"Yes." She blew her nose, then sniffed a little. "It was like I told you. Silver owned me. I was his property. I know he wanted me, but I wouldn't let him. He offered me money. He threatened me. He said I'd never work anywhere else. He wouldn't let me see people or go out. He...he even beat me up. I hated him." She was squeezing the purse again.

"But then, about six months ago, I met Charles Stevens. It was at the Silver Club. He was there with some people for a fundraising dinner. Silver had me entertain them. Then he told me that Charles would meet me later at the lodge and that I should be nice to him. But Charles wasn't like the others. At first, we just talked. Then he kept coming to see me. It was...different."

I looked at her carefully. "How different?"

"Not like that!" She glared at me. "Do you have to be so nasty?"

I shrugged it off. "What about Stevens?"

"He said he loved me." She tossed me a defiant look. "He said he was going to divorce his wife and take me away. I believed him. Only...." She slumped back in the chair, and the weariness crept back into her face. "Only now he's dead."

I stubbed out my cigarette in the glass ashtray on the nightstand. "Why come to me? Why not the police?"

"Silver would find me then. You're not from around here, so I thought you couldn't be mixed up with him." She paused, and her voice started to trail off. "I just didn't know what else to do."

I got up and went over to the window and pulled the shade aside just enough to see out into the street. A few cars went by, leaving wet tracks and a wash of road dirt. On the corner, a kid in dungarees, a pea jacket, and a dark wool cap was folding newspapers and stuffing them into a gray canvas carrying bag. As I watched, he reached for a rusty old bike that had been leaning against a lamppost. Then he hoisted the bag into a basket hanging from the handlebars, climbed on, and peddled off out of sight. Only the street was left, looking cold and damp and dark. That's the way I felt. I dropped the shade and turned back to the girl.

"I know there's more," I said. "If I'm going to help, you've got to tell me all of it."

She shrugged listlessly. "What difference does it make now?"

CHAPTER SIX

"You said Manelli used you in his business, at the motel?"

"Yes," she sighed. Her eyelids slipped halfway closed, and she stared idly at the window. "I made deliveries, packages. I never knew what was in them, but I could guess. The men would come from the club to see me, and afterwards they'd take the packages and leave."

"Did you ever take any packages to Stevens?"

"No!" She turned sharply. Then she looked down, reddened a little, and spoke quietly. "Yes. Just once."

"What was in it?"

"I don't know." She squeezed it out the way she'd been squeezing the purse. "Reefers, I think."

"That was all?"

"Yes."

"And with all these deliveries, they never gave you any money?"

"No." She looked up at me again, this time with a trace of interest. "How did you know?"

"It fits. They place their orders at the club and pay for them there. Probably even get a receipt for lunch or dinner. Maybe with some expensive wine, expensive enough so Manelli could afford to go to Italy to get it and bring it back. But it's still just bookkeeping for the Feds. He's just running a club; they're just buying a meal. Nothing changes hands."

I stopped and lit another cigarette. It tasted like burlap. Gloria was watching me now, not moving. I blew a lungful of smoke at the floor and went on.

"So, then they go to Shady Lodge to see you or one of the other girls. After they have their fun, they pick up their packages, pay the motel, and leave. There's no stash at the motel, and they don't give you any money. It's cute, real cute. If one of them gets pinched, all he did was rent a room. You just happened to be in it. You just happened to give him a package. It's all a big mistake. He's clean. If anyone's caught dirty, it's you. And there's no connection to Manelli. It fits all right. And it smells like last week's fish."

"That's about the way it goes," she said. "Ralph was right. You are smart."

"If I were smart, I'd be back In LA., swatting flies in my office. Or maybe

I'd be prowling the streets, playing tag with the junkies, chippies, and con artists. It isn't much, but I call it home."

"You sound bitter."

"I get that way when people try to set me up." I watched her. She began to gnaw on her lower lip. "Maybe you're not in on it, but I'm not in a mood to trust anybody. Frankie Bell saw me at Ryan's with Mrs. Stevens, so Manelli knew I'd be looking for her husband. Maybe he couldn't pin the killing on me, but he could hire me to get back some money that was taken from his club. Maybe I'd find you, and maybe the cops would nail me with a package of his dope. But he didn't count on my finding out that he was at the motel. So, maybe I'd just show up dead. Either way, I'm out of his hair, and he's even with me for blowing the whistle on his boys in Philly."

She put her hand up to her mouth, and her eyes widened. "My God. I shouldn't have come here. He might try to kill you too."

"Look," I said. "Let's say I'm just a chump. It's been said before. Let's say I believe you. Manelli isn't after you because you took a little of his money. And you wouldn't be irreplaceable at the motel. Sure, he's possessive. You told me that. And you look like someone a guy might leave home for. But not Manelli. He stays put. He might have it in for me, but he'd have Bell do his dirty work. He wouldn't move unless it meant a lot of long green. Or unless you had something on him. Right now, he's nervous—nervous enough to be in the motel room with Stevens and to have Stevens's office turned upside down. He's even nervous enough to play footsie with me for the time being, just in case I do find you." I watched her. Her eyes glistened with the hardness of ball bearings. "You took something all right. Was it one of his packages?"

She brought her hands together slowly and folded them tightly in her lap. The knuckles turned white and hard. She gazed at me for a long moment, with a question playing behind her blue eyes. Then it stopped playing. "You said you didn't trust anyone."

I nodded. "It's an occupational hazard."

"Charles told me not to trust anyone—anyone but him. He said it was the only way we'd stay alive."

CHAPTER SIX

"Good old Charles." I stood up. "Why don't we just forget the whole thing. Go and find somebody else not to trust." I walked over to the door and started to open it.

"Wait." She stood up and moved toward me. "Wait, please."

I waited.

Her eyes were very wide, and standing there, she looked even more drawn and pale. She opened her mouth, but before she could speak, she began reeling like a drunken sailor. I held her arms and steadied her, and guided her over to the edge of the bed. She sat down and put her hand up to her forehead. "I'll be all right. I haven't slept in…I'm not sure how long."

I sat in the chair and watched her some more. Finally, she put both hands on the edge of the bed and looked up at me. "You didn't know Charles. He was strong, confident. He made you believe him."

"I guess he got a little overconfident."

Her eyelids started to droop again, and she exhaled slowly, as if with great effort. "It was a book. I took it from Silver's office. Charles told me about it, and where to find it in Silver's desk."

"What kind of book?"

"It was small, about the size of a wallet. And it was filled with numbers, nothing else. I don't see how it could be so important."

"How did Charles know about the book?"

"I don't know. He said that so long as we had the book and kept it safe, Silver wouldn't bother us. He said that it would be like having an insurance policy. We could go away and live the way we wanted. So, one night between songs, I went up to the office. Silver was entertaining a bunch of his friends at the club. It was late, and they were all drunk. I only had a few minutes, but that's all I needed. The key to the desk was under his calendar, right where Charles said. The book was right there, in the back of the drawer. I took a quick look at it, but it didn't make any sense. Then I locked up the desk and went back downstairs. They never knew. I finished my numbers and went home. Next morning, I placed a classified ad in the paper. It was a signal for Charles. And I went to the motel and put the book under the mattress in the last cabin. Then I left. Charles told me not to go back there. He said he would get the book, but he wasn't sure when. He didn't want to go there on our regular day. He said when he had the book, he'd place an ad with a phone number where I could reach him. Until then, I had to hide."

"Where?"

"I stayed with a friend at first. Now I don't know. I went back to the motel late yesterday and hid in the main house. I didn't know Charles was there. I was there when you came in. And I saw Silver. He went into the cabin for a few minutes and then left. Then the police arrived, and there was a lot of commotion. Ralph came back and told me I could go, that no one would notice. He let me take his car. I met him this afternoon, and he said I should see you, so I came here." She bent forward and rested her head in her hands. "I can't go back to the motel now. I can't go home. And I don't dare go to the police. I just don't know what to do."

I went over to the nightstand and poured another drink. This time I didn't offer her any, I just drained it. Then I went back and sat down in front of her. "When you were at the motel yesterday, did you hear a shot?"

She looked up and shook her head.

"Did you see anyone else outside the cabin?"

"No. No one." She looked exhausted.

I sat back in the chair and eyed her for a minute. She had that street look of someone getting old in a hurry. The miles always added up faster than the years. I never knew one of them that was a good bet. I really must be a chump. I reached out and touched her hand, "Have you had anything to eat?"

All at once, she seemed to relax. "Not since yesterday."

I stood up. "All right. I doubt there's room service in this rat trap. But there's a cafeteria across the street. It'll just be sandwiches, probably give you indigestion."

For the first time, I saw the flicker of a real smile; only, it was the kind that comes at you from far away. I walked over to the door, took my coat off the hanger, and started to slip it on.

"You can stay here for now," I told her. "We'll talk some more when I get back. I still have questions."

She stood up and came over to me, and put her hand on my arm. Her eyes

CHAPTER SIX

were throwing a message at me that I didn't want to get. I'd seen it dozens of times before in one run-down hotel and gin joint after another. I really am a chump.

"Yeah," I said and took her hand off my arm. "Try to get some rest. And don't open the door for anybody."

I quickly slipped out, locked the door, and headed down the hall for the stairs. It seemed like a forty-mile hike. I tore down the stairs and out through the lobby like someone leaving a burning building. For the first time in a week, the cold damp night air felt good. I stood for a minute and just let it fill my lungs, then I started across the street.

On the corner, I noticed a phone booth. For once, I had some change in my pocket, so I dialed the operator and placed a long-distance call. There was a prim, official-sounding voice on the other end. Detective Rawls had gone for the day. Was there any message? I thought about giving her one, then I stopped. She wouldn't like it. Besides, I had Rawls's home number.

I went into the cafeteria and ordered three ham sandwiches and lots of coffee, to go. I could have ordered a three-inch, well-done sirloin in the twenty minutes it took. The waitress was the same one who served me breakfast. She looked at me kind of funny. They probably didn't have a lot of repeaters. Finally, she came out and handed me a paper bag that felt like a ton of bricks. I paid her, left an extra dime, and headed back across the street.

This time I noticed the lobby. There was no one behind the desk, and nothing moved. An old guy in an overcoat, rumpled pants, and shoes with holes in the bottoms was asleep on the couch. His hand was draped over the side next to some strewn sections of newspaper that rippled as his snores breathed under them. I tucked the bag under my arm and started up the stairs.

The radio was still playing somewhere on my floor, but it wasn't Glenn Miller. It was some kind of comedy show, the kind with a couple of characters talking and a lot of canned laughs. I wished that I could just go into my room and just sit down and relax. At least the couple across the hall had stopped fighting.

I unlocked the door and went into the room, and kicked myself. It was empty. I dropped the sandwiches on the bed and started to hang up my coat. Garrett, the great judge of character.

For just an instant, I could hear the sap whistle through the air. When it landed on the back of my skull, the world suddenly turned orange, and I was looking at it from a different angle, from the floor. Everything started moving around me. I became very busy trying to climb the floor, but it was too steep, and my hands and knees just didn't seem connected anymore. I could hear a thumping sound. I think it was my ribs. They were being hit by a pile driver, or maybe kicked by an elephant, or maybe it was somebody's shoe. I got interested in the floor again. It was friendly. It caressed me, cradled me. Finally, mercifully, it swallowed me up.

Chapter Seven

When you see it from the bottom up, a chair leg looks like a telephone pole. It was there, towering over me like a redwood. I blinked rapidly several times, trying to focus. I could see a dirty gray-brown sky full of indignant motion rushing around and over me. I drifted with it for a while. I began to notice that the sky was full of cracks, like a ceiling, and I was aware of something off in the distance taunting me. It was my stomach. It was unhappy.

I closed my eyes again, reached out with both hands, and with all my strength, I made the supreme effort. I rolled over. Slowly, I propped myself up against the bed, my knees nailed to the floor, and looked at the room. It was like seeing a carousel from the inside. When the room started to slow down, it began to hit me that I wasn't dead. I had a headache that went down to my feet, my ribs ached, and my mouth felt like the bottom of a birdcage.

The room was still moving a little, but I could see something dark and heavy in the middle of the bed. I steadied the bed with both hands. Then I reached out like a vagrant at a soup kitchen and carefully picked up my Luger. As bad as I was, there was no mistaking the fresh smell of cordite. The Luger had been fired recently. I dropped it on the bed again and fell back on my haunches. My stomach was starting to talk to me again. It was telling me to move, soon.

I pushed against the bed and tried to imitate someone standing up. Then I stumbled toward the bathroom and stopped at the door. She was sprawled across the tile floor, her head leaning against the wall next to the sink, and her arms and legs splayed like the spokes of a wheel. A dark wet stain had ruined the front of that inviting black dress and the body underneath. Her blue eyes were glassy, fixed on some unknown distance, and her mouth hung open as if trying to say something, only no one would ever hear it. What used to be Gloria Tempest was now just an unmoving heap of shattered flesh.

I stepped in and leaned against the door, and came away with a handful of blood and splinters. Two ragged holes the size of half dollars had been torn through the door, and they were smeared with splatters of red that had run down and started to drip into small pools on the tile. Out of some grim habit, I leaned over and put my hand against her neck. There was no pulse. I looked at my watch. Eight-thirty. I had left the room around seven. I decided that she must have been dead for at least an hour. She was lying in a red reservoir that had already started to gel.

Under the sink, there were at least a dozen scattered chips of tile. One of the bullets must have passed through her body and pounded into the floor. A Luger isn't like a Police .38 Special. The slugs don't just hit you, they bore in and keep on going. I looked at the holes in the door again. Whoever had used my Luger really meant business.

As I started to straighten up, the phone went off like a fire alarm. The impatient ringing tugged me out of the bathroom and across the miles to the nightstand. I sat on the bed and picked up the receiver, and just held it to my ear. On the other end was a voice like fingernails on a blackboard.

"Go back to L.A., Garrett. Nobody needs you here."

I recognized the high-pitched rasp, and my ribs were telling me they'd already gotten the message.

"What are you," I said, "the Chamber of Commerce?"

"Funny man. You got the word. Dust outta here before somebody stops your clock."

There was a harsh click and a lingering buzz. I hung up.

On the bed next to the nightstand, I saw one of the pillows wadded up like a boxing glove. I spread it out in front of me. The linen case was sharply creased and stained with familiar dark splotches, powder burns. Chances were that none of the other tenants heard the muffled shots. But even if some did, they wouldn't come around to investigate, not in this place.

CHAPTER SEVEN

For a minute, I just sat there with my hands on the edge of the bed. I closed my eyes and watched a swirl of unreal shapes and colors race past me, just out of reach. Then I snapped my eyes open again and looked around the room. My room. My gun. And a very dead lady who had given me some answers, but not enough. I looked across at the chair where I first saw Gloria Tempest. Something was different now. Beside the chair, next to the wall, was my suitcase, open, with some of the clothes tossed out and my only clean shirt dangling over the side. I got up and walked over, and stood with my back to the door, surveying the room. Two bodies in two days. Some batting average, Garrett.

I was only starting to feel human again when a fist began hitting the door like someone pounding a bass drum in the Rose Parade. I lurched around and yanked the door open, and stared into a large round nose surrounded by a puffy red-faced leer. It was Sergeant Moran. He was wearing the same tan trench coat, buttoned up and belted, and the same brown hat.

I stepped back and looked at him. I didn't think he was there to brighten my day. "You don't look like room service. Did you bring the ice pack?"

The leer faded into a question. "What for?"

"For what's left of my head." I sat down on the bed and gently rubbed the soreness extending above my shirt collar.

Moran came over and planted his hand on the back of my head as if he were squeezing a melon.

I winced. "Take it easy, will you?"

"Nice bump," he said. "What happened, you get sapped?"

"No. I just put my hat on too hard."

He straightened up and put on his best scowl. "Lieutenant Wells wants to see you, Garrett. Get your coat."

"Isn't that convenient. The request is mutual. Better have a look in there first." I motioned toward the bathroom.

He walked over and stood at the door, and looked in the same way I had. Then he let out a long, slow whistle and muttered, "Jesus!" He just stood there for a moment, not moving. "What a mess." Finally, be turned back to me. "Who blasted her?"

"Somebody who didn't want her to talk."

He walked over and stood by the bed. The scowl was gone, his face blank. "When did this happen?"

"She came to see me," I said. "We talked. I went out for a while and left her here. It must have happened then."

"Do you know who that is?"

"She said her name was Gloria Tempest. She was one of Manelli's playmates."

Moran pushed his hat back on his head and let out a soft, slow whistle. "She was his number one. He won't like this. I wouldn't want to be in your shoes, chum."

"They're old shoes anyway." I leaned forward and rested my head in both hands. I felt like a wet dish rag.

Moran picked up the phone and called the Station. He told them to send a team from homicide and to contact the coroner. Then he added, "And tell the lieutenant I got Garrett." After he hung up, he went back into the bathroom and looked around some more. I just sat there wondering if I could ever get my hat on my head again.

After a while, Moran came back carrying a small notebook and a pencil. He stood there scribbling. I was still enjoying my head. Finally, he put the notebook away and moved over to the bed next to me. He was about to say something, but then he stopped and stared at the bed. He pulled out his handkerchief and picked up my Luger, and sniffed the muzzle.

"Don't worry about prints," I told him. "I've already handled it."

The scowl returned, and his face began to flush. "What the hell for?"

"Sorry. I'm not at my best when I've been clubbed."

He waved the gun in my face. "Knock off the cute stuff, Garrett. Is this yours?"

"It's mine. Somebody fished it out of my bag." I pointed at the suitcase and my punished wardrobe.

"Somebody, huh?" His jaw set and a smugness began to creep into his voice. "What were you and the girl talking about?"

I let out a breath and stood up. "She was running from Manelli. She wanted

CHAPTER SEVEN

me to help her. We didn't get much past that."

Moran glanced toward the bathroom. "Some help. Why was she hiding?"

"She wanted to get away," I said. "Maybe she was tired of being Manelli's hostess."

"Why did she come to you?"

"Must have been my charming repartee."

He stepped close to me and grabbed a handful of my shirt, and bared his teeth in my face. "Look, Garrett. You're in a bad spot, so cut the crap. If you don't come clean…."

Before he could finish, there was another rap on the door, but lighter than his had been. Moran opened it and let in Ferris and two other men. One was carrying the usual coroner's black bag. I watched them. For small-town cops, they always seemed to arrive in a hurry.

Moran pointed across the room. "In there, boys. It's a messy one."

The three of them crowded into the bathroom and went to work without saying anything. Moran turned to me. "All right, Garrett. Let's go."

He reached up and jerked my coat off the hanger, and pushed it toward me. I just got my hand on it when something wrapped in brown paper slipped out of the sleeve and thudded at my feet. Moran bent down and picked up a package a little smaller than my fist. He kneaded it a few times, testing the contents; then he looked up at me with an eyebrow raised. "What's this?"

I didn't think he really wanted an answer, so I just stood and watched while he pulled out a pocket knife and poked a small hole in the paper. He shook a sprinkle of white powder onto his palm and then tasted it like a cat licking milk from a saucer. The leer began to rise on his face again, and he stuffed the package into his pocket.

"Well, well," he said happily. "Look what we've got. Here you are with a dead girl in your room, probably killed with your gun, and a stash of junk in your coat."

"You left out the dirty laundry on the floor."

This time he laughed. "Keep It up, Garrett. The lieutenant's gonna love this."

Chapter Eight

Another ride downtown. I was afraid it might become a habit. Moran ushered me into the same corner office and parked me in the same wooden chair. Lieutenant Wells was out; I'd better just wait and behave myself, he said. I decided not to argue. Moran left, and I looked around the office. It hadn't changed much. Cops' offices never do.

The minutes passed by, but not in any hurry. I listened to the wind outside. Every now and then, it caught the tall panes of glass behind the desk and vibrated them in their ancient wooden frames, producing a hum like the sound of a rubber band stretched tight. It gave me a hollow feeling, like hearing a train whistle off in the distance. I thought about how I'd been sitting in Lacy's only a week ago, listening to some soft, warm music. I missed the music. I missed the warmth.

Wells came in and moved briskly behind the desk. He was wearing charcoal-colored trousers, a white shirt with the sleeves up, and a pale blue tie at half-mast. He sat glaring at me, his dark, stubbled chin and furrowed forehead almost leaping across the desk. He looked like a cop, an angry cop.

"You couldn't take a hint, could you?" he demanded. "I told you to get the hell out of here."

I nodded. "You told me. But I still have a client." I reached up and rubbed the back of my head. "And I'm developing a fondness for your town."

"Well, the feeling's not mutual. You're operating here only because I let you. And that's only because you know Ed Rawls." He read my expression like a tout with a racing form. "That's right. I called him. He says you're square, but I don't see it yet. So, you'd better make me believe. Tell me what

CHAPTER EIGHT

happened to Gloria Tempest."

"She showed up in the wrong place."

"Yeah. But not by herself." He sat up in the chair. "She comes to visit you and takes four slugs from your gun. Her coat and purse are stuffed in your closet. And we find you holding a bag of heroin. I could add it up that you killed her."

"Sure," I said. "You've got it. I shot the girl with my own gun in my own hotel room, planted the junk in my coat, and then I sapped myself on the back of the head just to make it look good. You shouldn't have any trouble making that stick."

He slumped back in the chair and exhaled deeply. "Okay, chump. I know it's a frame. You had no motive. Moran told me you took a hard bump. And the lab boys said that the dope was cut with so much flour it couldn't have brought anything but pin money on the street. It was just enough to make you look dirty, but not enough for a real motive. So, who would want to set you up?"

"It had to be Manelli. He tried to hire me today. He said he wanted me to find Gloria Tempest."

Wells folded his hands together against his chin. "That's why you were at the Silver Club?"

"That's right. You got eyes there?"

He put a sour eye on me. "None of your business. What makes you think it's Manelli? It's not a good frame. He'd have to know it wouldn't stand up."

"Maybe he just wanted to rattle me. He was after the girl, and he saw a chance to use me. When she showed up, he knocked her off, or his ape did. After I came to, I got a call from Frankie Bell telling me to blow town. They wouldn't have bothered if they wanted me dead. Manelli's a friendly guy, great sense of humor. Maybe he thought he could make me look bad, hurt my business. Cases are hard enough to get these days. It could be his way of evening the score with me for fingering the Hinsons." I wasn't sure he'd buy that.

"Okay. Let's say I buy that. What was Gloria Tempest doing in your room?"

I pulled out a cigarette and lit it, and let the smoke slowly drift across the desk.

"It's like I told Moran," I said. "She came to see me. She was hiding from Manelli, and she wanted my help."

"But why you? What could you do for her?"

"She seemed to think I was clean, not connected to Manelli or to you. Ralph, the kid at Shady Lodge, steered her to me. Ask him."

Wells leaned forward and put both hands flat on the desk. "I'd like to. But I can't. We found Ralph tonight floating face-down in the creek behind the lodge. There was a wire wrapped around his neck that cut all the way through his larynx."

I could only stare at him. Wells lifted a hand and brought it down on top of the desk with a sharp slap.

"Damn it, Garrett. He was one of ours. We planted him there six months ago to get the goods on Manelli. Now, thanks to you, Ralph is dead, and I have to start over. So, you'd better start playing ball, or so help me, I'll lock you up so tight your shadow will need a separate cell." I felt as if my ribs had just been kicked again.

Wells folded his hands on the desk and took a couple of deep breaths. He held his dark eyes on me, and I saw them start to settle and harden. It was like watching a lake freeze over. When he spoke, his voice had the steady, even tone of a professional.

"We know you went to see Ralph today, that you put some muscle on him. What for?"

I crushed out my cigarette in the wastebasket. "I didn't believe his story about not seeing anybody around Stevens's cabin. He admitted that the girl was there. And he saw Manelli's car. Nice of you not to tell me."

Wells sat back and pressed his lips tight together. "I don't owe you anything. Besides, all we have on Manelli is circumstantial. We can't prove that he killed Stevens."

"Did Ralph tell you that Gloria Tempest was at the motel when your boys put the arm on me? Did he tell you that she'd been there for a while and that she saw Manelli?"

"No." His eyes widened a little, and the furrows tightened.

CHAPTER EIGHT

"Ralph had more than just a business interest in Gloria Tempest," I said, "only I don't think she gave him a tumble. But he was sweet on her enough to keep her hidden. And after he realized I was working on my own, that I had no strings, he told her to come and see me. She saw Manelli enter and leave the cabin. She didn't know Stevens was in it."

Wells suddenly clenched both fists and pounded on the desk. "Son of a bitch! An eyewitness, and she's dead. Is that why Manelli wanted you to find her?"

He watched while I shook another cigarette out of the pack and lit it. I offered him one. He accepted it and took a deep drag without taking his eyes off me. I went on.

"I don't think so. He probably didn't know that Gloria had seen him. And at least until this afternoon, he still trusted Ralph. He told me that Gloria had stolen some money from his club. She said she didn't. I believed her. She wasn't as tight with Manelli as he wanted people to think. She said she and Stevens were going away together. Stevens was connected to Manelli in some way. I don't know how."

I watched Wells's eyebrow jump up slightly. But he still didn't move.

"I figure Manelli knew that Gloria was playing around with Stevens, and he's got too much vanity to let that get out. After all, he's the boss. He owns everything. What's more, if word got around about disloyalty in his organization, another mob might think he was getting weak. Maybe they'd try to move in. Manelli knew Mrs. Stevens had hired me. Maybe he figured I could track down Gloria and keep it hushed. With the two of them out of the way, Manelli gets rid of a problem in his organization and keeps his reputation intact. He rubs out a girl that he wants and can't really have, so no one else can have her either. And he even has a little fun with me. People have been killed for less. You said she was shot four times?"

Wells nodded.

"She was shot at close range," I said, "by someone in the room. A pro wouldn't need more than one shot, two at the most. Judging from the holes in the door, he hit her twice on her feet and twice when she was down. That's not a professional hit. That's revenge, maybe jealousy, maybe both. You still think Stevens's death was a suicide?"

Wells exhaled slowly and let his hands fall in his lap. "I never did. I just wanted you out of the way so you wouldn't wreck our setup." He leaned his head back against the chair, gazed at the ceiling, and then turned toward me. "What are you going to tell Lenore Stevens?"

"She hired me to find out what happened to her husband. I figure she's paying for the truth. Only I don't have it all yet."

"So, what are you going to do?"

"Maybe I'll go and visit Manelli. After all, he did offer to double my fee to find Gloria."

"What about Frankie Bell?"

"Oh, yeah." I rubbed the back of my head. It was still sore. "I'll make time for him, all right."

Wells put on a grim smile and slowly shook his head. "All right. You can go, but I'm keeping your gun as evidence. I'll have Moran drive you back to your hotel. Only this time, I'm telling you to stick around. Whether you're still working for Lenore Stevens or not, don't leave town. You're not clean yet."

I got up and started for the door. As I grabbed the knob, I looked back at him. Wells was standing behind the desk, his hands shoved into his pockets. "Never mind," he said to me. He turned toward the window. "Just be careful."

I felt cold again. I had told him the truth, or most of it. I left.

Sergeant Moran drove me back to the hotel with the enthusiasm of cold soup. He stopped at the curb and waited while I got out.

"Keep your nose clean, Garrett," he grumbled. I gave him a line about his own nose, and he drove off.

It was getting late, but somehow I wasn't tired. I got into the DeSoto and headed down Central to Route 12, and turned off at Shady Lodge. The place was deserted, no cars, no lights, no business. The police had sealed up the last cabin with a pair of two-by-fours nailed across the door and the only window. I used the jack handle from the car as a lever and pried off one of the boards. After that, it took me less than a minute to jimmy the window

CHAPTER EIGHT

and slip inside.

The room was the same, but this time the bed was empty. I switched on the light on the nightstand and lifted the mattress. There was a tired-looking mesh of bed springs, an old section of newspaper, and dust enough to wade in. But there was no book. I replaced the mattress and checked the rest of the room. I went through the dresser, closet, and bathroom. Nothing. I turned off the light and went outside, and replaced the board by pounding the nails back in with my shoe. As I drove back toward town, my thoughts played hide-and-seek. Three people had been in that room. Two of them were dead.

It was just after midnight when I turned off Central onto Steiner Street. It was mostly residential, with more rowhouses, apartments, and a dry cleaner on the corner. The sidewalks were scraped clean, and the rain had washed away most of winter's icy remnants, revealing small patches of bare gray turf. Number 712 was a three-story brownstone about half a block down from Central. It had a long-suffering look. A lone streetlight glared over a streaked and weathered brick front, and the smudged windows showed an assortment of drab shades and curtains, all drawn. A half-dozen cement stairs led to an entryway in the middle of the first floor, with a small foyer at the top lighted by a single overhead bulb. I got out and went up the stairs. It seemed a long way from Shady Lodge.

The front door was locked. It was one of those electronic locks that you activate from inside if you like the sound of the voice over the intercom. On the wall next to the door was a row of mailboxes with push buttons over them. I punched every button. After a while, a voice sounding like a second-grade teacher assaulted me over the speaker. "Who is it?" I didn't answer. "Who's there?" It sounded like an order. I moved into the corner out of the light. There was a pause, and then the door began to buzz.

I moved quickly through the door and stood in a plain corridor facing a flight of stairs covered by a faded green carpet and sided by a dark wooden banister. I heard a door opening somewhere above the stairs and then footsteps. The old lady was waiting for her caller. I held my breath for what seemed like a couple of hours, and finally, the footsteps started again and receded, and the door closed. I went back to breathing.

There were only two doors on the first floor, so I headed upstairs on tiptoe. Number Four was one flight up. There was no police seal on it. Wells's boys hadn't had time to rifle the place. I used a nail file to spring the lock. Two minutes' worth of manicure, and the door was open. I stepped into a small hallway, shut the door, and reached for the light switch. A ceiling lamp with an opaque glass cover tossed an indifferent light on Gloria Tempest's apartment.

It looked like a place that someone had left in a hurry. The central living room was small and square, with doors left and right. The wood flooring was partially covered by a thin coffee-brown carpet that was almost held in place by a settee and two chairs that might have been left over from Herbert Hoover's parlor. Each piece stood on walnut legs that curved like dollar signs, and the upholstery on the seats and arms was covered with a smooth plum fabric fastened by brass-headed tacks.

On the far wall, a single window was masked by cream-colored chenille drapes. In front, a small circular table was held up by a wooden pedestal. A pot-bellied smoked-glass lamp sat on the table, trying to hold on to a flaring ruffled shade. An assortment of books and magazines was carelessly piled on the floor in the corner next to the fragments of a porcelain figurine. Not very tidy.

I stepped through the door to the left into a kitchenette that felt as roomy as a crowded subway. The cupboards were all open, the drawers were pulled out, and the contents were spread across the counter and piled in the sink. In the corner, I saw the remains of a broken Blue Willow plate. I picked up the pieces and tossed them into a waste basket under the sink. Garrett, the homemaker.

I crossed back through the living room and went into the bedroom and found about what I'd expected. The bed was unmade, and the bureau next to it was partly open, showing some rumpled undergarments and several sweaters. In the far corner was a white vanity table with a few lady's oddments scattered on top. As I approached it, I was stung by a familiar hint of jasmine. I remembered the girl sitting in my hotel room. And I remembered how much

CHAPTER EIGHT

my head still hurt.

I checked the bathroom. It was empty, except for a pair of nylons hung over the shower rod. There was nothing in the medicine chest, so I went back and looked in the bedroom closet. There were only two or three dresses, a flannel suit, and a pair of brown open-toed high heels. Not much left. And there was no luggage.

As I turned back toward the bed, I noticed a brown leather-bound scrapbook lying on the floor like a man spread-eagled on his stomach. I picked it up and sat down on the bed, and began thumbing through the pages. It started with yellowed snapshots of Gloria as a child and a younger girl that must have been her sister. Then there were newspaper clippings and publicity photos showing Gloria Tempest, the promising Philadelphia nightclub singer. Tucked behind one of the clippings was half of a snapshot that had been torn down the middle. It showed Gloria standing in front of what looked like a cafe. She was wearing a plain sweater, and slacks, and her hair hung loose. She was smiling, but her eyes had that same faraway expression.

I looked around the room again and slowly let out a breath. It always happened that way. When you're running, you don't have time to pack your memories, not even the good ones. I tucked the picture into my pocket and walked back into the living room, and just stood there. Something wasn't right. It could have been me.

I took my handkerchief and went back through the apartment, wiping the prints off everything I had touched. Then I switched off the overhead light and poked my head out into the hall. There was no one there and no sound. The hallway was holding its breath. I remembered that Wells had my Luger. It was probably the right thing. All I'd do is shoot someone with it.

I quietly shut the door behind me and eased my way down the corridor. My shoes made a crinkling noise on the carpet that echoed off the walls like the beat of a snare drum. I made it to the head of the stairs with nobody chasing me. It would have been easy to go down the stairs and leave, if only she hadn't been standing in my way.

Chapter Nine

"Hello, Handsome." She stood there, her tails and net stockings showing below a reddish-brown twilled coat trimmed with black fur. Even in the dim light of the hallway, I could see the yellow sparkle of her boyish-cut hair. Her green eyes had streaks of light that moved like grasshoppers on hot pavement. I could make out a smooth oval face with thinly rouged cheeks, a gently sloping nose, and dimples. And she had that high-priced smile, the kind that makes men out of boys and boys out of men.

"Hello, Daphne," I said. It was as good a line as any.

She stepped up to the top of the stairs and stood next to me. She smelled of back rooms and cigar smoke. "You're tall," she said.

"I used to be taller. I'm out of practice."

"What're you doing here?"

"Looking around," I said. "I do that for a living."

She angled her head to one side. "'That's right. You're looking for Gloria." She giggled. "I wish you were looking for me."

I let that one pass. "Do you live here too?"

She nodded. "A lot of the girls from the club do. It's a quiet place. No problems, if you know what I mean."

I knew what she meant. "I should have checked in here." I looked at my watch. It was just twelve-thirty. "Aren't you home early?"

"It was a slow night. Silver and Frankie were both out." Her eyes widened, and she pointed her smile at me. "Say, why don't you come in and tell me all about being a detective?"

CHAPTER NINE

"Why would you want to know that?"

She took my arm and began leading me up the hall. "Because I like the way your mouth moves when you talk."

She opened the door to number six, across the hall from the apartment I had just left, and we went inside. She peeled off her coat and hung it in a closet by the door. I gave her my hat and trench coat. She eyed them like a customs agent looking for fruit flies.

"Pour yourself a drink, sweetheart," she said. "It's over there." She pointed to a small Mediterranean-style cabinet in the corner on the left past the sofa. "There's ice in the fridge. It'll only take me a minute to change." I watched the tails on her jacket disappear into the bedroom.

The apartment layout was the same as Gloria's, but that's as far as it went. The furniture was modern, squared off, and low. There were only two pieces you could sit on. In the corner to the right, a tall philodendron drooped forward like a vulture eyeing a fresh kill. It hovered over a love seat that faced across the room toward the sofa. Both pieces were covered in a sateen peach fabric that appeared to be blushing. I could see why. On the wall over the sofa was a print of a Renoir nude the size of a billboard. The place was as subtle as an air raid.

I walked across the room to the cabinet, making my way through a white shag carpet that must have had a standing appointment at the local beauty shop. I found a bottle of Vat 69 and two glasses. I poured about two inches and drained it. It slid down like honey, so I poured another and looked around some more.

Under the window was a glass-top table with wire legs like coat hangers and a telephone on it. Next to the phone was a tall lamp, the kind that's not supposed to look like a lamp. The thing had a chrome spiral stem with a crystal globe on top. The globe was covered with strips of chrome, leaving a few narrow slits for the light to worm its way through. I switched it on. A little light slipped out, about as much as from a candle on a birthday cake. But it was enough for me to read the name on the envelope that was lying behind the phone. It said, "Daphne Croft." I looked inside and saw a handwritten note. It read: "Garrett. L.A. private. Pilgrim Hotel." And it had my room number. I went over and sat on the sofa. I felt as naked as the girl in the picture.

Daphne floated in wearing her smile, and a long black clinging satin robe with large felt-covered buttons on the front. She must have worked hard getting the robe almost buttoned.

"You found the Scotch," she said.

"It wasn't hiding."

I watched her as she filled a third of a glass and took a deep swallow. She went over to the door and flipped off the wall switch, leaving only the strands of light coming from the table. As she moved back across the room, her impatient figure began to wrestle with the robe. It was no contest. The robe was overmatched. She poured her curves onto the sofa next to me and took careful aim at my libido.

"I'm glad you dropped in," she said. "We really couldn't talk when you were at the club."

"All work and no play," I said, just so she could watch my mouth move.

She reached over and started to loosen my tie. "Why don't you get comfortable?"

I took her hand and pushed It away. "People have been making me comfortable all day. What do you do at the Silver Club?"

"I wait on tables." The corners of her mouth curled upward. "And on people."

"At Shady Lodge too?"

"Now, don't be ugly." She stuck out her lower lip in a playful pout. Then she wrinkled her nose and leaned over against my shoulder. One of her buttons fell conveniently open, giving me a glimpse of her all-too-available figure.

"So, your name is Michael," she said. "Do they call you Mike?"

I shook my head. "Never."

"I'm glad," she purred. "I think I'll call you Mickey. I like that better than Mike."

"How do you know so much about me?"

"Silver told everyone about you. He said you were going to do something

CHAPTER NINE

for him." She traced a finger along my neck and behind my ear. "He said we should be nice to you."

I stood up and moved over in front of the lamp. "How nice?"

She grinned and tossed out a low throaty chuckle. "Mickey, darling."

She glided off the sofa in my direction, almost leaving the robe behind. She pressed close to me, the contours of her body making an impression my suit would always remember. She curled her fingers around the back of my neck and breathed close to my face. "We could have a late supper…and breakfast."

I pushed her back to arm's length. I could have bounced her off the wall. Women were coming at me from every direction.

"What did Silver tell you about Gloria Tempest?"

A clouded look moved across her face, and she dropped her arms to her sides. "You're no fun."

"What about Gloria? How much fun was she?"

She shrugged and let out a sigh. Then she went over and stood by the loveseat, facing me.

"Gloria and I have never really been close. We get together and chat over coffee sometimes, but mostly she keeps to herself."

"Chat about what?"

The smile crept back. "About men, lover. What else?"

"What men?"

"Only the good-looking, rich ones." She giggled again. "I hope you're rich."

"Yeah, of course," I said. "I have the butler read the want ads to me every morning. Is 'Gloria Tempest' her real name?"

"I don't know. Most of the girls do use phony names. But, in this business, it doesn't pay to get too personal. Gloria's never said anything about it, and I haven't asked." She paused and hid behind a suggestive smirk. "Would you like to know my real name?"

"I don't think my blood pressure could stand it. What do you know about Charles Stevens?"

She frowned and gnawed on her lower lip. "I only saw him at the club. He was there a few times with some lawyer from Philadelphia. They'd come in, sometimes with a crowd, sometimes not. Silver always set them up in style.

It was good to work then. The tips were big."

"Just tips?"

Her green eyes flashed, and she moved closer. "Why, Mickey. Are you jealous?"

I skipped that one too. "Did Stevens ever come here to Gloria's apartment?"

She stopped and pondered. "No." Then her forehead fretted a little. "Why are you looking for Gloria?"

"It's the in thing to do these days. Has there been anyone in her place recently?"

She thought some more. "No, I don't think so. Why?"

"And of course, you wouldn't know. That would be getting too personal." I stepped toward her, and she sidled back toward the loveseat and said nothing.

"When was the last time you saw her," I asked.

"About a week ago, at the club."

"Did she say anything about leaving?"

"No." She looked down. "But I guess I'm not surprised she's gone. She hasn't been around here much since she started seeing…him."

"Yeah." I moved over in front of her. "You know that Stevens was found dead yesterday?"

"Yes," she said quietly. "I heard. Poor Gloria. I think she was really hooked on him."

"She was hooked all right, hooked on payoffs and promises." I watched her eyes widen. "You can skip the hearts and flowers, darling," I said. "She's dead."

"What?" Her mouth dropped open. The smile was gone.

"I found her tonight in my hotel room, shot with my gun."

She turned away from me and pressed her hands together. "Oh, no. Not that. Not her."

I spun her around and held her arms tight against her sides. "Why not her? Why not me?" She writhed against my grip. "Manelli told you to be nice to me. Did he tell you to visit me at my hotel?"

"No." She flashed me a green glare and bared her teeth. I didn't care. I went at her again.

CHAPTER NINE

"It was a great setup, Daphne darling. Whoever shot Gloria sapped me and planted a bag of dope in my coat. A real sweet frame. Just the kind your boss would think of."

She stopped struggling and slowly shook her head. "He…he wouldn't."

"Wouldn't he? I think you know he would. For somebody who keeps to herself, you know a lot. You know about Gloria. You know about Charles Stevens. You know about me. I think Gloria did talk to you. You could have tipped off Manelli. What did you get for it, a free fix?" I pulled up her sleeves and looked at her arms. No marks. "Maybe not. Maybe you just got a night off from the lodge."

She threw a look at me that I hadn't seen since they tossed me off the force. "You bastard." She yanked her arms free and snarled at me. "Get out!"

"Sure." I moved toward the door. "But if I were you, I'd be careful. People who talk to me seem to wind up dead. Just ask Ralph." I reached into the closet and put on my coat and hat. "On second thought, you can't. Ralph's dead too. He was killed tonight, garroted mob-style. You travel in real friendly circles, darling."

She stood frozen, her face the color of the carpet. There was something in her eyes that I hadn't seen before. It was fear.

"So long, lover," I said, and closed the door behind me.

I walked quickly up the hall, making a week's worth of noise. At the head of the stairs, I paused and slipped off my shoes. I crept back quietly and put my ear to the door at number six. It was a kid's trick. Kids can be smart. Daphne was talking on the phone.

"He was just here…. No…he must have found your note…. All right, all right. I'll be more careful…. Yes, I'm all right…. No. He didn't say anything about it. I'm not sure he knows…. She couldn't have. I checked…. Yes. I know." She cleared her throat. "No, please. I can't. He's…. Yes. I understand. All right." She hung up.

As I slipped back through the hall and down the stairs, I heard a door close. I felt like kicking it down. I put my shoes on and left.

By the time I got back to the hotel, the police had cleared out. The lobby was empty. Even the old man on the couch had gone. I took my bottle of Old Kentucky from the car and went up to my room. There was no sound, and I didn't get hit on the head.

The boys from the Lancaster police lab had been just tender enough with my room. Except for the window shade, everything had been dusted, pulled apart, or turned over. The only chair was left facing the wall, the bed was stripped down to the mattress, and the lamp and nightstand were covered with enough powder to smother an elephant. My suitcase and clothes and all my toilet articles had been dumped on the bed. I looked in the closet. I found the bag from the cafeteria, torn, and three ransacked sandwiches.

I went over to the window and stared out, listening to the wind fill up the night. The cafeteria was dark now. In the cold glow of the streetlight, I could see the bare branches of a lone elm tree stretching up behind the cafeteria. The branches moved in the wind with a desperate reaching, like a cramping swimmer about to go under. Beyond the tree, I could make out the shadowy hulks in a junkyard that spread across the next block. Down there in the twisted metal, I could almost see the relics that had once cruised the streets, bright and clean and new. I saw myself among the shadows.

I turned away and took out the torn picture of Gloria Tempest. Someone had been in the picture with her, someone who was torn away like the rest of her life. And there was lettering on the dark glass front of the café. I couldn't make it out. I studied her face. She was giving me that unspoken message, the same one she gave me before I left her. The picture felt electric.

I stripped off my coat and shirt and went into the bathroom to wash some of the grunge off me. The police had left a chalk mark on the floor, outlining the position of the girl's body. I didn't need the reminder. I stepped around the mark and stood straddling it in front of the basin. She'd been stepped on enough. I looked into the mirror. Something looked back, gray and dark and ugly. I splashed cold water on my face and toweled it off, and looked in the mirror again. The thing was still there. I'd had better nights.

I went back into the bedroom, crammed my clothes back in the suitcase, and threw a sheet over the bed. Then I checked the nightstand, hoping to buy myself a drink. Moran hadn't missed that either. The bottle was

CHAPTER NINE

empty. I pulled the pint out of my coat and poured myself about three inches of consolation. It wasn't as smooth as the Vat 69, but it was friendlier. I stretched out on the bed in my undershirt and sipped slowly. I looked at the door. I looked at the wall. I looked at the ceiling. I looked at the door again. I looked at my watch. Almost two. Rawls might still be up. I placed the call.

He was up all right, and not happy. "What the hell have you been doing?" he raged. I let him go on. "Wells called and chewed on my ass. He says you fouled up a caper he had planned to bag Manelli. He said that a girl from the club was killed in your hotel room and that you fingered a kid he'd planted at the motel and that the kid got bumped too. Damn it, Garrett. Everywhere you go, there's trouble. Why can't you just keep your nose out of things?" He stopped to catch his breath.

"Have you blown enough, or do you want to yell some more?"

"You bastard." He'd had enough.

"How about letting me just tell my version?"

"Go ahead," he grumbled.

"I was set up for a frame. The kid Wells planted at the motel was soft on the girl. He tried to get me to help her, trying not to tip his hand, only somehow Manelli found out, and the kid got chilled. When the girl came to see me, I walked into a sucker play and got hit from behind. She was shot with my Luger, and there was a bag of heroin planted for the cops to find. Nothing pure, just back-street stuff. I talked to Wells. He knows it was a frame."

Rawls just grunted. I could picture the dour set of his jaw. He had grunted at me before. I asked him. "Did you get anything on Stevens's business?"

He let out a long slow sigh. "I talked with some old friends in the D.A.'s office in Philly. Charles Stevens was president of the Wheelright Foundry. He was also president of Stevens Associates. It's a privately owned corporation, a holding company that also runs a loan operation, mostly backing small businesses in eastern Pennsylvania. They actually own Wheelright. The foundry got a lot of wartime business. Since then, not so much. But the loan business must be good. Stevens Associates always seems to have money to lend."

"That fits," I said. "The foundry didn't seem too busy. Anything else on

Stevens Associates?"

"Not much. Their major stockholder is a Chicago company called Mid-States Development. I couldn't get anything on them, except they're involved in real estate and investments."

"Who's in charge in Chicago?"

He hesitated. "I don't know. But there may be a way to find out. Mid-States is represented by an attorney from Philadelphia named Mark Halstead. He's with a firm called Caulfield and Sanders."

"Anything else?"

"No." He cleared his throat, and his voice softened. "How's Lenore?"

"I've seen worse. She's taken a lot. Her husband was involved with that girl who was killed tonight. So far, I don't see any cracks."

"She was always a classy lady." He was drifting into some long-forgotten yesterdays.

"Listen, Eddie," I said. "It may get worse. Stevens was mixed up with Manelli's operation in some way. There's prostitution in it and drugs and something more. I don't know what."

"Damn," he said. "What's that going to do to Lenore?"

"I don't know. But from the look of things, Stevens wasn't the competition, you thought. You should have stuck around."

"You bastard."

"That's what they're calling me tonight. Thanks, Eddie." I hung up.

I poured the rest of the pint into my glass and sat there on the bed. My head still hurt, and my legs felt like wet timber. I thought about Daphne Croft lying to me with her body. I thought of Lenore Stevens touching my arm, her brown eyes filled with a silent pleading. And I thought of the ocean touching the beach at Malibu up the coast from L.A. It was early morning. The air was crisp, and the breakers were throwing a quiet foam on the sand. Suddenly I could see Manelli. I could feel his icy sneer coming at me from behind his desk. It gave me the shivers. I took a deep slug and stood up.

I picked up the picture of Gloria Tempest again. I thought of her talking to me, and I thought of her lying on the floor in the bathroom, not talking. I put the picture back on the nightstand and poured down the rest of my

CHAPTER NINE

drink. Then I hurled the glass across the room.

Chapter Ten

There were fish in it. Small, darting, frightened fish crowded my dream. They flitted around me, pausing for a desperate moment. Then they swished away, leaving a curtain of bubbles. I could see faces in the bubbles, faces from present and past, faces I knew, yet didn't. They were gaunt, fearful, and they all stared at me, pleading in silence. Then the bubbles drifted away, and I felt the fear. Another fish was moving toward me, a big silver fish. It had red eyes and gaping jaws, and it was swallowing the other fish with a kind of cruel pleasure. The eyes fixed on me, and the jaws widened almost into a smile. I began swimming away. But the big fish kept advancing. I swam as hard as I could, yet it moved nearer and nearer. The eyes flashed, and the jaws widened even farther. From deep inside the fish, I could hear a mocking, rattling laughter. I awoke with a jolt and was drenched in sweat.

I sat up quickly and swung my legs over the edge of the bed. Somewhere off in the distance, I heard my feet hit the floor. I rummaged on the nightstand for a cigarette and rolled it around in my mouth without lighting it while I looked out the window. The sky was covered with tall shifting clouds, layered white on gray. They moved above the town like people crowding into an elevator, bunching and jostling. I could hear the wind racing past the window. It spread dust and scraps of newspaper up the street, and it made ripples on the few pools of rain left standing on the pavement. The street was empty. The town was quiet. Charles Stevens was being buried today.

I struggled up from the bed and made my way to the bathroom. My head had stopped hurting, but my ribs were stiff and sore. I studied them in the

CHAPTER TEN

mirror. They looked medium rare. I took another lukewarm shower and managed to shave without losing too much blood. I thought it might be pressing my luck, but I got dressed and headed across the street.

The cafeteria was the kind of place you go to only because it's there. It had a grimy glass front that made it hard to see inside. That was just as well. Inside, a row of booths stretched across the front and down the left wall. Each one had padded seats, covered in cracked red plastic, and Formica-topped tables about the same color as the window. To the left of the counter, there were more tables surrounded by wooden chairs with the same red plastic seats. A counter with a ridged metal ledge and a stack of trays on the end faced the door. Behind it was a row of square metal steam trays, each holding something molten. A cash register was parked on the end of the counter at the left, with a sleepy-looking plump woman perched on a stool behind it. She was about thirty-five, and her image was topped by yesterday's blond hair framing baggy eyes. The place did a lot for your appetite.

As I stepped through the door, I noticed a thin character in an underfed topcoat and gray snap-brim hat hiding behind a cup of coffee in the corner booth. When he saw me, he ducked down behind the cup, leaving his hat showing above the folds of his coat.

I got myself some coffee and left a dime for the girl at the cash register. Then I went over, slid into the booth, and sat looking across the table at Officer Ferris. He sat stiffly, looking back at me. There were a few dozen boney fingers wrapped around his cup, and his pale yellow-green eyes scanned me from beneath his hat brim.

"Are you going to drink that coffee or squeeze it to death?" I asked him.

He slowly unwrapped one of his hands and lifted his cup, and took a couple of slow-motion swallows. Then he replaced the cup and made a noise at me through his teeth.

"You're a crumb, Garrett."

"I could almost get the idea you don't like me," I said.

"Go to hell!"

The muscles twitched along the ridge of his jaw, and a large blue vein stood out on the side of his neck. The dark leathery skin, deeply creased, fell over his boney features like a collapsed tent. His thin pointed nose reached out from between a pair of sunken cheeks that made deep shadows under his eyes and gave the rest of his face a run-over look. Watching him, I felt almost human.

"Is that any way to talk to a guest?"

He scowled into his cup for a minute, then brought his eyes up to mine without disturbing the scowl. "I wouldn't be doing this, but they told me to watch you."

"That should be easy. I spend a lot of time floating in coffee cups."

His upper lip curled into a snarl. "Lay off, gumshoe. You could go back to L.A. in a box."

"That's not a very friendly approach."

He put a stranglehold on his cup again. "Listen, Garrett. You're gonna get hurt."

"The same as Gloria Tempest?"

He brought one of his hands up over the table and curled the fingers into a fist that looked like knotted barbed wire. Then he held that fist up in front of my face.

"This is what you get," he said. "Not like her. She took it the easy way. There wasn't a mark on her. You're gonna look like a roadmap of Pittsburgh."

"She'll be glad to know how easy it was."

The anger trickled out of his face. I watched him settle back in the seat and squeeze the edge of the table with both hands.

"Did anyone in the hotel hear the shots?" I asked.

He reached up and slowly pushed his hat back off his face, revealing a salt-and-pepper widow's peak. "Nope."

"Where was the manager?"

"Out."

"And nobody saw anything?"

He just stared at me, a go-to-hell smirk trying to play at the corners of his mouth. I took out a cigarette, perched it between my fingers, and leaned across the table.

"Look, Ferris. Until you show me different, I take you for an honest cop.

CHAPTER TEN

You might even be good at your job. I've been a sleuth for a while, and I've been around some. I don't think you like seeing people killed any better than I do. And I know you've got no reason to give me any real heat. So, let's skip the Dead-End Kids act."

The smirk disappeared, and he just sat there staring. He looked disappointed. He took a slow breath and eased his hands up onto the table.

"I don't have much," he said. "We talked to a kid, a paper boy. He was out here last night." He motioned toward the window. "He saw the girl go inside while he was folding his papers. She was alone, she didn't talk to anybody, and she seemed in a hurry."

"Is he sure?"

"We showed him the body. He couldn't identify her, but he recognized the blue hat and trench coat. He fingered her all right. But Moran still has doubts."

"Yeah," I said. "I'll bet he does. Did the kid see anybody else?"

"That's it, just the girl."

I lit a cigarette. "You boys gave the room a dusting. Any prints?"

"Only from you and the dead girl. And we checked everything. Moran said to cover the place good." He finally gave me something resembling a grin. "Moran pegs you for trouble. He told me when he called the station that there was a hit in your room and that we should take the place apart. He said I should bring our best boys. He said if you were involved, we damn well didn't want to miss anything. Don't want it to look like we're railroading the L.A. dick, he said. Took me a while to round up our boys. Had to make a couple of extra stops. And we spent a long time in your room. But Moran insisted. He said if you did it, he didn't want you slipping off the hook. And if you didn't do it, he wanted to be sure of that too, so we can get after whoever did." He seemed pleased with himself. "You've been a lot of work for me."

I took a deep drag on the cigarette and blew the smoke at the window. "What does Moran think now?"

"Like I said, he still has doubts. It looks like you were set up. But there's no evidence of any third party. So, he says we keep an eye on you."

"He says?"

He took his hands off the table and adjusted his hat back down on his head. "Look, Garrett. I don't always agree with Moran. He gets into it sometimes. But he's a good cop. Besides, we all take orders from Lieutenant Wells."

"Not all of us."

His fingers began tensing, and he edged forward in the seat. "Don't try anything funny, Garrett."

"I wouldn't think of it." I slid out of the booth and stood up. "Does this town have a hall of records?"

"Yeah, sure." He raised a quizzical eyebrow. "It's in the Municipal Building."

"Is it open on Saturday?"

"I think so."

I offered to let him ride with me, but he grumbled and said he had to go back to the station. He gave me directions, and I wasn't heartbroken to leave without him.

My next stop was the liquor store for some more Old Kentucky. The same old man looked at me kind of funny.

"Where are you putting it?" he asked. "Gasoline rationing's over."

"I've got a sick friend," I told him.

"You must not want him to get better," he said.

I didn't say anything.

As I carried the bottle out to the car, I spotted a pawn shop across the street. I went in and found a thin dark character wearing a green eyeshade. He had a Smith and Wesson .38 caliber for sale. I gave him cash. He didn't ask questions. I got into the car and tried out the Old Kentucky. The old man might have been right about my sick friend.

Chapter Eleven

The Municipal Building was a square stack of red bricks just a block and a half south of the police station on Fort Street. It had tall casement windows that may have been washed once, and it was fronted by a stubby brown hedge that had been hacked down almost to the sidewalk. Three brick steps led up through a break in the hedge to a set of glass-paneled double doors. A cement slab with carved lettering reading TOWN OF LANCASTER, 1912 was fastened over the doors, and on either side of the steps was a cement urn holding the remains of something that must have stopped growing when Calvin Coolidge left office.

I left the DeSoto across the street and ran through a biting wind up the steps and into a small, tiled lobby. There were two doors straight ahead, a narrow stairway to the left, and on the wall to the right, a directory. The Department of Records and Vital Statistics was on the second floor. I went upstairs.

I clicked my heels up a tiled hallway, went through the only door, and stood in a room that took up the entire second floor. Rows of green filing cabinets crowded the sides and back of the room, covering the lower half of the windows. They all faced two long wooden tables and about a dozen empty wooden chairs lined up crisply in the middle of the room. Across the front was a chest-high wooden counter, with a latched swinging gate to the right of it and a woman standing behind it.

My suit would have been small on her. She had a couple of inches on me in height, and she was built as solidly as the building. Her long black hair was piled up on her head like a haystack, and a pair of dark bushy eyebrows hung over a face that looked like a shovelful of wet plaster. Her round pulpy nose was parked above a wide wrinkled mouth that had a thin ridge of dark hair across the upper lip. And her chin was long gone, surrounded by two puffy jowls and a ruffled collar. She wore a dark dress and an expression to match.

"You want something?" She had a voice like a bullhorn.

"I'm here for the fifty-cent tour."

"Look, buster," she said. "We close at noon, so this is a short day for me. Don't make it any longer."

I told her I wanted to look up some business permits. She puffed up her jowls and leaned on the counter. "You'll have to do your own digging. I'm the only one here today."

I looked around at the empty room. "I'll try not to disturb anybody."

She snorted and led me around behind the counter, and pointed to the wall on the left. "That's it. You can use one of the tables. Just be out of here by noon."

There couldn't have been more than a dozen cabinets. The permits were filed by date, alphabetically. After only forty minutes and two cabinets, I had some luck. In 1946, permits had been issued for the Silver Club and for Shady Lodge. Both were for standing structures, and the applications had both been made by Capital Investments Corporation of Chicago. There were no names and no records on the Chicago company. The permit for Stevens Associates was filed under the same year. It was listed as "general finance," and it showed Mid-States Development, also of Chicago, as co-owner with Charles Stevens of Lancaster.

It took almost another hour, but finally, I found Wheelright. The foundry had been bought out of receivership in 1938 by Charles Stevens for fifty-five thousand dollars—more than I could afford, but not much for a wartime industry. There was a note stapled to the card saying, "See purchase, 1946." I went back to the second cabinet and found that Charles Stevens had later sold the foundry to Stevens Associates for almost three times what he paid for it. I spread the permits out on the table in front of me and reflected for a minute. 1946 had been a big year.

CHAPTER ELEVEN

I put the permits back in the file. Then I went up to the counter and told Sparkle Plenty that I wanted to look at individual certificates and licenses. She looked as if I'd just asked for her life savings. Then she snorted again and pointed to the cabinets on the right.

There was no birth certificate for Charles Stevens, but there was a marriage license dated 1943. It listed Charles J. Stevens, born 1913, parents John and Frances Stevens of Philadelphia. He was marrying Lenore Parker of Lancaster, born 1916, parents deceased. I looked for her birth certificate. It wasn't there. Just on a chance I looked for the records on Gloria Tempest and Santino Manelli. Again, I came up empty.

I closed up the files and turned back toward the counter. I was wondering where else I might look, when Lieutenant Wells came through the door. He was wearing a gray tweed topcoat, a gray hat, and lots of worry lines. Without breaking stride, he came around the counter and through the gate and marched up to me.

"Are you taking over for Ferris?" I asked.

He reacted as if I hadn't said anything. "I heard you were here. There's been a burglary at the Stevens house. I'm on my way there. You want to come along?"

I nodded. He turned and headed back toward the door. On my way out, I stopped and looked at the woman who had welcomed me earlier. She was spread all over a chair behind the counter, giving Wells a crusty eye. She turned and looked at me.

"So long, dear," I said. "It's been a pleasure." She snorted. I left.

We went up Main, turned onto Flint, and headed for the suburbs. Wells drove with both hands on the wheel, clenching and squeezing as if he might get water out of it. We rode for several miles before he began to talk.

"It was the butler that called us. He said they came home from the funeral and found the downstairs torn apart."

"Don't they have an alarm in that house?"

He nodded. "But Rogers said it was turned off. He said they don't use it much, only when no one's there. In the confusion over the death and the funeral, Mrs. Stevens forgot to turn it on."

"Did they see anybody?"

"I don't know. He said Mrs. Stevens had gone upstairs. He sounded pretty rattled."

"Rogers? Never."

Several minutes passed. Wells looked straight ahead and kept twisting the wheel. Then he tried again.

"Ferris said you spotted him first thing."

"It wasn't easy," I said. "He had a great disguise."

He glanced over at me quickly, then turned back toward the road. "You may not know it, Garrett, but I'm trying to keep you out of a jam."

"Thanks, but I'm a big boy now. I tie my own shoes and everything."

"Yeah," he said. "I know you like to play it by yourself. But Manelli's a tough customer. You get in his way, and he'll feed you to the fish without thinking twice."

I didn't say anything. I didn't want to think about fish again.

"Look," he went on. "Rawls and I go back a ways. I heard about your trouble ten years ago. He said they never really pinned anything on you and that he thought you were on the square."

"Yeah, that's me. Clean as Shirley Temple."

He chuckled quietly. "He also said you wouldn't give an inch." He turned and looked at me. "But I figure maybe we can help each other out."

"Maybe," I said, "if you call off your boy scouts."

He turned back and moved his mouth around as if he were chewing on an idea. "Okay, I'll take off the tail. Can you give me anything?"

I inhaled deeply and watched the houses roll by the car window.

"Nothing solid. Stevens was connected to Manelli, but you must know that. He may have been killed because he was trying to break that connection. There may be something in his financial organization. He made a killing buying the foundry and then selling it back to his own company. And there's some kind of tie-in with a Chicago company called Mid-States Development."

"Never heard of them," he said. "But I'll have the Chicago boys check. You think there's a link to Manelli?'"

CHAPTER ELEVEN

"Maybe." I hesitated. "Ever hear of a Philadelphia mobster named Petrone?"

His jaw set, and he squeezed the wheel tighter. "Everybody who's worked in Philadelphia knows about Anthony Petrone. He was the big racket boss there in the twenties and thirties. They say he had Chicago connections. He was into everything. Booze first, then gambling and prostitution. Manelli started working the street for Petrone, and he moved up very fast. Some said, too fast. He was Petrone's lieutenant for almost ten years. Word was he was really running things. Petrone was getting old, ready to retire. Manelli was just waiting. Then somehow, in early 1940, they got into a dispute. Manelli was cooking up something that Petrone didn't like. Petrone ordered a meeting of the heads of the northeast families. The story goes that he was going to give Manelli the big kiss-off. But the meeting was never held. That morning Petrone was found in his car, parked in front of his nightclub. He was wearing a Chicago necktie, like Ralph. His house was burned down, and his family gone. Then Manelli took over. No one challenged him."

"That's a lot to get away with, even in the mob."

"Yeah," he said. "But it's been that way ever since. Nobody bothers Manelli."

"Somebody's bothering him now."

He looked over at me and seemed ready to say something. But instead, he turned back toward the front of the car and just managed to miss one of the brick pillars at the end of the Stevens driveway. We drove up to the front of the house and parked between a black Packard sedan and a racy green Hudson Hornet.

We got out and headed up the steps. There was sunlight showing on the porch, but the wind was lacing the shrubbery, making it crackle. It was a blistering wind, the kind that leaves you with a dry taste. I turned up my coat collar, and Wells rapped on the door.

The knocker was still bouncing when Rogers jerked the door open. He threw his arms forward and looked at us as if the house were on fire.

"Lieutenant, Mr. Garrett, I'm so glad you're here. Mrs. Stevens has been hurt."

Chapter Twelve

Rogers wrung his hands together nervously, his eyes showing a lot of white.

"I heard her scream, and I ran upstairs. She must have walked in on him in the bedroom. I found her on the floor, and the balcony doors were open."

I followed Wells into the entrance hall. "All right, Rogers," he said. "One thing at a time."

Rogers squashed his lips together and busied himself with our hats and coats, while I looked around. It wasn't hard to see why he was upset. The umbrella stand was lying on its side next to the table. Scattered around it were the shards of a crystal vase that had been knocked over and some mangled carnations; the tapestry rumpled, the corner folded under next to the wall. The Chinese guy was still hanging up there sucking on his pipe. He didn't seem to mind the mess.

Wells looked over at me, then turned back to Rogers. "What happened?"

Rogers drew himself up, still holding our coats in an untidy bundle in front of him. He took a deep breath. "In all my years of service, nothing like this has ever happened. Martha and I returned from the funeral with Mrs. Stevens late this morning. As you can see, we found the house in terrible disarray. The drawing room, the kitchen, this…" He motioned over his shoulder. "I've never seen anything like it."

Wells gave him a patient nod. "Please go on."

"Well." He cleared his throat. "Mrs. Stevens told me to call the police while she went upstairs to see if there was any more damage. I directed Martha

CHAPTER TWELVE

to begin cleaning up the drawing room, and then I phoned your office. Just as I was hanging up, I heard Mrs. Stevens scream, and I ran upstairs." His breathing was starting to shorten.

Wells put his hand on the man's arm and spoke in a voice as calm as a glass of warm milk. "I'm sure this is difficult for you. Just take your time."

Rogers lifted his shoulders and inhaled again, remembering his composure. "Yes. Well, I found Mrs. Stevens in the bedroom. She was slumped on the floor, holding the side of her face. I asked her what happened. She said that a man attacked her and that he went out over the balcony when he heard me coming."

"Did you see this man?"

"No, sir." He hesitated. "That is, not exactly. I went out on the balcony and saw a man, a very large man, run across the backyard and go through the hedge."

"Could you identify him?"

"No, sir. I only saw him for a moment and from behind. But as I said, he was very large, and he was wearing a brown leather jacket."

A knot began creeping into my stomach. "Is Mrs. Stevens all right?" I asked.

"I don't know," he said. "She seemed dazed at first. I called Dr. Ramsey immediately. He's with her now, in the drawing room."

I told him we wanted to see her.

"Yes, sir. If you'll just wait here a moment." He turned and carried our coats through a doorway by the stairs.

Wells turned toward me, showing the beginnings of a frown. "Just let me ask the questions. Get it?"

I didn't say anything. I was thinking about what I was going to tell Rawls.

Wells was about to say something when Rogers strode back into the hall. He moved with the deliberate gait of someone in charge again. He nodded curtly and said, "This way, gentlemen."

We followed him across the hall and into the drawing room. It was pretty well roughed up too. Most of the books had been pulled off the shelves and tossed around the room. The oriental rug lay in a heap, bunched up next to the sofa, and one of the blue stuffed chairs was tipped over against the fireplace. The portrait of Charles Stevens was still there, but it was tilted to one side. I studied it for a minute. Even sitting at an angle, he seemed to be staring at me, accusing me. Nice going, Garrett, he was saying. Still a step behind.

The other chair and sofa were sitting almost where I remembered them. Martha must have started her straightening up there. I looked at the chair. There was a man in it. He was no more attractive than the average matinee Idol, about thirty-five, with wavy black hair and the deeply tanned features that a lot of women would want to take home, and probably did. His face was broad and smooth with a prominent chin, straight nose and mouth, and pale green eyes with black centers that caught the light like drops of oil. He was wearing a double-breasted, charcoal-gray suit with extra-wide lapels and pencil-thin, chalk-white stripes. The trousers held a crease sharp enough to shave with. A crisply folded white handkerchief, carefully placed in his breast pocket, matched the glimpse of white shirt that just managed to show behind a quiet gray silk tie. The only thing missing was a price tag.

He sat facing the sofa, casting a practiced look of concern on Lenore Stevens. She was sitting there looking up at another man. This one was older, fifty-five or sixty. He had a short, stocky frame, a thicket of close-cropped white hair, and a reddish, square, unmoving face. He was wearing a navy-blue suit with a vest stretched across a prosperous stomach. He stood in front of the sofa, his thumbs hooked into the pockets of his vest, and he was leaning slightly forward, nodding.

"The dizziness will pass," he said. "Just rest and try to avoid any excitement for a few days."

Rogers stepped up to the end of the sofa. "Lieutenant Wells and Mr. Garrett, madam."

Lenore Stevens stood up and turned toward us. She had on the same cream-colored robe I remembered from the night before. Only now, she looked very different. Her hair was pulled around and draped over her right shoulder, revealing the long slender curve of her neck and an angry red welt that covered her left cheek and the outside of her left eyelid. As I moved

CHAPTER TWELVE

closer, I could see the currents moving in her brown eyes. They showed uncertainty and fear, but mostly anger.

"Oh, you're here," she said. She looked over at Wells. "Lieutenant, this is an outrage."

"Yes, ma'am," Wells said discreetly, looking over at the two men. "Perhaps we can discuss it." He was good.

She straightened, and I watched a calm recognition run down her face like melted wax down a candle. "Of course," she said. "I'm sorry to be so abrupt." She was good too.

She pushed out her arm in a polite sweep, aiming it at the older man. "Lieutenant, Mr. Garrett, this is Dr. Ramsey." The man bowed at the waist and sent an unapproachable "How do you do?" toward Wells. Then she motioned toward the chair. "And this is Mark Halstead." The matinee idol just nodded, his eyes fastened on me.

Wells stepped up to the sofa and spoke to the doctor. "I hope Mrs. Stevens isn't seriously hurt." It was his way of asking the question.

"No. A bit shaken, as anyone would be. A nasty business. But she's a fine healthy young lady." Ramsey gave Lenore Stevens a reassuring nod. "An excellent physical specimen." I wasn't sure if that was for her benefit or his.

He took her hand in both of his. "I'll be going now, my dear. Remember, get plenty of rest, and take one of those tranquilizers if you awaken during the night. Call me in a day or two." He excused himself and left, disappearing into the hall with Rogers.

Wells turned smoothly and spoke to the other man. "Mr. Halstead, what's your interest in all this?"

"I'm the family attorney, Lieutenant." He had a deep rolling voice that stopped Wells in his tracks.

Lenore Stevens interrupted. "He's also a good friend."

"I was at the funeral," Halstead continued. "And I came here afterward. I arrived shortly after Mrs. Stevens."

"Did you see the burglar?"

"I can't be sure, Lieutenant." He stood up from the chair and straightened his suit as if he were about to go on stage. "But I did see a car just as I was turning in at the driveway. I wouldn't have paid any attention, but it came around from a side street and went right past me. It was going very fast. I thought there might be an emergency." He hesitated. "I'm afraid it didn't occur to me to get the license number."

"What kind of car was it?" Wells persisted.

"Well, actually, it was a Checker cab."

Wells threw me a look you could read from across the street. He turned back to Halstead. "Then what?"

"Then nothing. I came to the house and met Rogers at the door. He told me what had happened. Lenore came downstairs. The doctor arrived. And we came in here to wait for you."

"Lieutenant," Lenore Stevens spoke again. "Mr. Halstead is a good friend of the family, and he's been a great help and comfort to me, making the funeral arrangements and all. But none of us expected this. We just didn't know what to do."

"I understand," said Wells. "There's really nothing much you could do." He looked back at the idol. "Thank you, Mr. Halstead."

"Not at all, Lieutenant. I only wish I could be of more help." He turned back to Lenore Stevens. "Lenore, I'm afraid I must leave too. If you need anything, just let me know."

"Of course, Mark," she said sweetly. "And thank you for everything."

Wells's forehead began to wrinkle. "Where can we reach you, Mr. Halstead, just in case we have more questions?"

"I'll be at the country club. I'm staying in one of the guest cottages until tomorrow night. Then I'll be going back to Philadelphia." He produced a small brown leather folding case, pulled a card out of it, and handed it to Wells. "Please, Lieutenant. Feel free to call me any time."

Wells took the card. "That I will, Mr. Halstead."

Halstead reached over and gave Lenore Stevens a perfunctory hug. She responded the same way. Then he nodded to Wells, painstakingly ignoring me, and moved out into the hall like John Barrymore making an exit.

Lenore Stevens motioned to Wells, then to me. "Lieutenant, Mr. Garrett, please sit down." She sat down on the sofa while Wells parked himself in

CHAPTER TWELVE

the chair where Halstead had been sitting. I pried the other chair off the fireplace, righted it, and sat in it.

Wells began right away. "Mrs. Stevens, I'm sure this is difficult, but I have to get all the facts. Can you tell me what happened?"

"First, Lieutenant, let me apologize. I shouldn't have snapped at you." Her expression was softer now. "You're right, it's been a difficult time for me. And to come home to this." She tossed her hand in the direction of the mess behind her. "I'm sure you understand."

"Yes, of course. If another time would be better…"

"No," she said. "This is perfectly all right." She sat upright and folded her hands in her lap. "We came straight back here from the funeral. Rogers and Martha rode with me, and Mark—Mr. Halstead—followed us in his car. When we arrived, we entered the house through the garage and went into the kitchen. Right away, we saw that someone had broken in. The French doors were smashed, and there was glass all over the floor. We walked into the hall, saw the damage there, and then we came in here and found this." She began rubbing her hands together. "I was very upset. I thought it was vandals, people who take pleasure just from breaking things."

"Was anything else torn up like this?" I asked.

"No, not downstairs. I told Rogers to call the police, and I went upstairs to see if there had been any further damage. I checked the guest rooms and found nothing. Then, as I entered the master bedroom, I saw a man." She took her hands and spread them tightly over her knees. "He was standing in the closet, looking through my clothes. I must have made some noise, because he turned around and saw me. He started toward me, and I screamed. Then he grabbed me by the arms and shook me, hard, and demanded money. He yelled at me, 'Where is it? Where is it?' I screamed again, and that's when he hit me." She curled her hands into fists and squeezed them white. "He kept hitting me." Her eyes became moist. "Then suddenly, he stopped, and I fell to the floor. I guess that's when Rogers came in. The man simply went out onto the balcony and climbed over the railing." She opened her fists and seemed to relax. "Rogers helped me up onto the bed and then called Dr. Ramsey. About that time, Mark arrived. The rest you know."

Wells spoke to her. "Mrs. Stevens, are you sure you're alright?"

"Yes, Lieutenant." She began slowly stretching her fingers. "I was pretty fuzzy at first, but I'm all right now."

"Do you keep any valuables in the house?"

"A little money and some jewelry. Nothing terribly important."

"Was anything stolen?"

"I'm not sure, Lieutenant. I'll have to let you know."

Wells hesitated. His question sounded almost like an apology. "Mrs. Stevens, did you recognize the man who attacked you?"

She began tensing again. "No. I've never seen him before."

"Can you describe him?"

"Not very well, I'm afraid." She chewed on her lower lip for a minute. Then she leaned forward and began moving her hands in front of her as if she were shaping a snowman. "He was very large, with a brutish face, and he had dark red hair. I remember that. And he was wearing a brown leather jacket." She paused for a moment, then let her hands fall limply in her lap. "That's all I can remember."

Wells was about to say something, but I got my question in first. "Did he say anything else?"

She looked at me and blinked. "No. He just said, 'Where is it?' I assumed he wanted money."

I had another question, but Wells reached out and put his hand on her arm. "I'm sorry to put you through this."

She bent her head and spoke quietly in the direction of the floor. "It's all right. I'm more embarrassed than hurt, really." She looked up and exhaled almost with relief, like someone finishing five years of hard labor. I put my question away.

"Charles was always so strong," she went on, "so much in control. I wish I could be more like him. I suppose there are burglars who follow the obituaries, looking for homes to rob." She looked down again. "Perhaps I should have had someone here. At least I should have remembered to turn on the alarm. Charles would be so disappointed." She looked up once more. This time her voice was firmer. "But it's my responsibility now, and I'll deal

CHAPTER TWELVE

with whatever comes. Don't worry about me, Lieutenant. I'm all right." I thought about Rawls again. At this point, I wasn't sure what to tell him.

"It might still be a good idea," said Wells, "having someone here."

"But why?" she asked. "Surely he wouldn't come back."

Wells stood up and walked over to the fireplace, and put his hand on the mantel. "Mrs. Stevens, from your description, the man who attacked you is one we want for questioning in connection with the death of your husband." He read the expression on her face. "That's right. We've ruled out suicide. We think your husband was murdered."

Her jaw dropped, and she looked over at me. Her brown eyes glistened. She looked back at Wells. "But why?"

"Well, first of all," he went on, "because the circumstances were unusual. Most suicide victims don't drive all the way out of town to kill themselves. They do it at home. Second, there was no note. With the kind of man your husband was, with all his business involvements, chances are he would have left word for someone. That's all speculation, of course. But then on top of it all, this case just has too many connections."

Her eyes were riveted to him now. "What connections?"

Wells folded his arms and spread his feet, like someone preparing to deliver bad news. "There was a connection between your husband and a woman who worked for the owner of the Silver Club, the same man who runs Shady Lodge. His name is Manelli. He's a gangster we've been trying to nail for years, and he's connected to a man who fits the description of the one who broke in here and attacked you. His name is Frankie Bell. He was spotted at Shady Lodge by Garrett here the night your husband died. And he may have been involved in the killing of a woman named Gloria Tempest in Garrett's hotel room last night."

Her hands flew up to her face. "Oh, dear God." She looked at me, then back to Wells, her eyes even wider. She moved her mouth, but nothing came out.

Wells started again, his brows sharply creased and his voice a tone higher. "That's not all. A young man named Ralph was killed at Shady Lodge yesterday afternoon. A young man that your Mr. Garrett leaned on. The young man was working for us. We think Bell may have done that one too."

THE SILVER SETUP

Lenore Stevens slowly brought her hands down from her face, her expression unchanged. "But Lieutenant, what would such a man want here?"

"That's what I want to know," he said. "Right now, he's the only common link we've got in three killings. The only one, that is, except your Mr. Garrett." He motioned toward me. I felt like ducking.

There was a silence as heavy as a millstone. I watched Lenore Stevens. She clenched her teeth and folded her hands in her lap, carefully, deliberately, like a judge about to pass sentence. Her eyes hardened as she looked at Wells. The anger was returning.

"Lieutenant, I know my husband was having an affair with that Tempest woman and that she worked at that gangster's nightclub. And from what I've heard about Shady Lodge, anything could happen there. None of this is the result of my hiring Mr. Garrett. When you came here yesterday, you said I'd made a mistake hiring him, that he would simply get in your way. Now you're implying it again. Well, Lieutenant, even without Mr. Garrett, I can't see that you've done very much. My husband was murdered in that awful place, and you say one of your own people was right there. His office was ransacked, my home broken into, and I was attacked. And now you tell me you know who did it." Her eyes were flashing now, and she threw her words at him like darts. "Lieutenant, why isn't this Bell person in custody?"

"He will be," Wells replied calmly. "I'm sorry to upset you, Mrs. Stevens."

"Very well, Lieutenant." She set her jaw firmly and continued to glare at him. I could see a deep flush creeping up the side of her neck. I stood up.

"Mrs. Stevens," I said, "if it's all right with you, I'd like to have a look around upstairs."

She just looked at me and nodded.

"I'll try not to get in your way." I nodded to Wells and headed out. Wells followed me, leaving Lenore Stevens burning on the sofa. We climbed the stairs without talking.

The bedroom was messed up, but not as much as the downstairs. The four-poster bed was rumpled, as if someone had slept in it. Next to it on the nightstand, the frilly shade of a small brass lamp was sitting at an angle. But the lamp was still upright. I got down on all fours on the thick white carpet

CHAPTER TWELVE

and looked under the bed. I didn't find anything.

Wells walked across the room and opened a pair of louvered double doors, and went out on the balcony. As I was climbing up off the floor, he called back to me over his shoulder. "Garrett. Out here."

I walked out behind him and looked at the backyard. It couldn't have been much bigger than a football field. It stretched out straight from a small patio underneath the balcony, and it was ringed by tall, thick evergreens standing shoulder to shoulder. Even with the grey-brown look of winter, the lawn seemed as well cared for as the infield at Yankee Stadium. The patio was also ringed by evergreens but trimmed down short enough to see over. One of them was partly bent over and broken.

Wells pointed to it. "Bell must have landed down there and then run over to that side street." He pointed to the left. "He would have left his cab there so he could come in through the kitchen."

I looked at him for a minute. "Why? No one was home. He could just drive up to the front door."

"Maybe he was afraid of Mrs. Stevens coming home and walking in on him, just the way she did."

"Maybe." I looked out over the yard. It was still early in the afternoon, but the clouds were moving in, filling the sky with a cold dark purple. The wind came across the balcony and stung my face like a Joe Louis jab. I turned up the collar on my suit jacket and looked back at Wells. "Maybe he just likes running through backyards."

Wells shrugged out a sigh. "Look. I've had people out looking for Bell since yesterday, when you told me you saw him at Shady Lodge. And I've had people watching this house."

"But he wouldn't know that."

"Oh hell," he said. There was irritation in his voice. "What do I know? Manelli isn't dumb enough to pull a stunt like this. Bell could have broken from him and gone out on his own. So maybe he squeezes the local merchants for whatever he can get and makes a quick hit here before he lams out of town. He's probably hiding from Manelli as much as from us. That's why he wouldn't use the front door. His phone call to you last night could have been to keep you off balance and give him a little more time. You said yourself it could be a warning."

I turned my back to the wind and folded my arms against my chest. "Maybe. But there are three dead people, Wells. Bell's had his chances. So, why haven't I come up number four?"

He cracked a dry smile. "Maybe Bell figures that with you alive, I'll have my hands full keeping you out of trouble." I just looked at him, and his smile faded. "We'll get him. I've put Moran in charge."

"Yeah," I said.

My eyes were starting to water from the wind. I turned and went back into the bedroom. Wells followed me. We walked over to the far side of the bed and stood in the closet doorway. The closet was filled with women's clothes, shoes, and hats, all out of some fashion magazine. I thought about the empty closet in Gloria Tempest's apartment.

Wells whistled. "Boy," he said. "These duds had to cost plenty. I wonder what Bell wanted here."

Across the back, high up, a wooden shelf was struggling to hold a few dozen hatboxes. Most of the boxes had been opened, and a collection of plumed and feathered hats tossed around, some falling on the floor. I reached down and picked up a plain, rounded, blue-gray hat with a wide brim that was crumpled up in the corner under some shoes. Then I picked up a black brocade beret. It had a long quill stuck to the side of it and a circle of rhinestones in the middle. One hat would attract a lot of attention. The other wouldn't. I held them up in front of Wells. He just shrugged. "Try figuring women and clothes," he said.

We stepped away from the closet and looked over the dressing table that stood between the closet door and the bathroom. There were several jars of creams and an assortment of bottles with an assortment of smells. Nothing was overturned. Nothing seemed out of place.

I followed Wells to the bedroom door. He went out into the hall and started toward the stairs. I stood there for a minute and looked back, rubbing my thumbnail across my front teeth. Something was bothering me. Wells came back and tapped me on the shoulder. We went downstairs.

CHAPTER TWELVE

Lenore Stevens was waiting for us at the foot of the stairs. She had cooled off some, but she still seemed edgy. "Lieutenant, I'm terribly sorry. I didn't mean to be cross with you. I know you're just trying to do your job."

"That's all right, Mrs. Stevens. I understand."

Rogers appeared with our hats and coats, and we made motions to leave. But then she spoke again.

"Mr. Garrett, could I speak with you for a moment, please?" She paused slightly. "Alone."

I looked over at Wells. "Go ahead," he said. "I'll wait for you in the car." He and Rogers moved toward the door, and I followed Lenore Stevens into the drawing room.

She stood in the middle of the room with her back to me. Her shoulders shuddered. Then again. She was crying. I reached out and touched her arm, and she turned and looked at me, tears rolling down both cheeks.

"Oh, Mr. Garrett," she said. "I'm so frightened."

"I know. I'm frightened too."

She put her hand against my chest. "Is it true what Lieutenant Wells said? Were those people really murdered?"

I nodded, "It's true." I could see the fear in her eyes. And I could see something else. I wasn't sure what it was. Maybe a longing. "Mrs. Stevens, this is important. Did your husband ever say anything about Gloria Tempest?"

She looked down and shook her head. "No. Never." There was a hint of bitterness. "Charles was always very discreet about his…affairs."

"Did he ever mention a book, small, maybe the size of a wallet. It may have had something to do with your husband's business."

She shook her head. "Charles hardly ever discussed business with me. I'm sure he never said anything about a book. Why is it so important?"

I looked at her for a minute, hoping she could take it. "I think Frankie Bell's looking for something. It could be that book. I think he came here trying to find it." I motioned with my head toward the mess on the floor. "This wasn't an ordinary burglary. It's just supposed to look that way."

Her mouth dropped open, and her fingers began clutching at the front of my shirt.

"He probably didn't find what he was after," I said. "You interrupted him."

Her breath caught, and she brought her hands up to her face. "Can this really be happening? That terrible man? What if he comes back? What will he do?"

I put my hands on her shoulders. "He won't come back. I'll see to it." I wasn't sure why I said that. Or maybe I was.

She stared up at me, trying to blink the fear out of her eyes. "I'm so glad Edward told me to call you." She lifted her arms up and around my neck and squeezed hard, resting her head against my shoulder. She clung to me like a small child. I put my arms around her. The soft scent of her hair rose and wrapped itself around me. I could have held her for a week.

"Ed told me to look after you, to keep you from getting hurt. You mean a lot to him. It won't be easy. There are some rough characters to deal with. And there may be some ugly publicity. But I think you'll be safe here for now. And I'll try to get Wells to keep the lid on."

She lifted her head and looked up at me. "I don't think he trusts you."

"He's right not to trust anybody in this business. I don't."

She squeezed again and pressed her cheek next to mine. "Be careful."

I pried myself loose and stepped back, and looked at her. I could see why Eddie cared so much. "I'll be back later." I turned and walked out into the hall.

Rogers met me with my hat and coat and walked with me to the door as I put them on.

"Did you hear anything besides a scream?" I asked him. "Any noise or talking?"

"No, sir. Just the scream. As soon as I heard it, I ran upstairs immediately." He shook his head. "Such a shame. First poor Mr. Charles. And now this. They've always been such a fine couple, such a pleasure to work for."

"Yeah. Too bad they didn't get along."

"I beg your pardon, sir?" He raised an eyebrow.

"Never mind. It was probably a private matter."

"Yes, sir." He shook his head again. "Poor Mrs. Stevens. I can't imagine

CHAPTER TWELVE

what she'll do now."

    I looked at him for a minute, then I looked back toward the drawing room. I could still feel the strands of her hair brushing against my face. I turned and went out the door and down the steps. The wind was still gusting hard. Somehow it didn't seem to bother me.

Chapter Thirteen

Wells drove me back downtown without saying much. When we pulled up behind the DeSoto, he rested his hands on the wheel and looked at me. "Okay, Garrett. Spill it."

"Spill what?"

"Listen, we both know that Bell didn't break in there just to pull a heist."

"Yeah? What about Bell leaving Manelli and skipping town? That was smooth. You know people don't leave him and go on breathing. You didn't believe that line any more than I did."

He flashed a quick smile. "Maybe I just wanted to see some of your detective brilliance."

"Sure," I said. "People think that private detectives are all men like Sam Spade and Philip Marlowe. They just hold up a cigarette and wink, and a couple of gorgeous babes are right there ready to cuddle. Then between drinks, they solve the crime as if any kid could do it, and almost without a single clue. That's not the way it works, pal. You know that. There are always too many clues, pointing in too many directions."

"I just figured you California guys had all the answers."

I turned and stared out through the windshield. "Not in this weather."

"All right. No more kidding." His voice was quiet, measured. The smile was gone. "I think you've been holding out on me. I think Frankie Bell has been trying to find something. That's why he tore up Steven's office yesterday. That's why he broke into the house today." He leaned toward me in the seat. "And I think you know what he's looking for."

"Suppose I do?"

CHAPTER THIRTEEN

"Suppose you get your head blown off? Whatever they're looking for, they're killing people to get it. I think that phone call from Bell was to warn you off, so you don't find it before he does." His forehead wrinkled, and he gave me a too familiar scowl. "I figure you're holding the key to two, maybe three murders, and that's something I want. Now give."

I let my breath out slowly and looked at him. "First, I want something."

He just kept scowling.

"I want Lenore Stevens kept out of it. No heat. No publicity."

He sat back and softened his furrows. "That's a tall order. But for her, I don't mind trying."

"And I want you to keep your shooflies off me."

He hesitated.

"It's that, or I stay clammed."

He nodded.

So, I lit a cigarette and told him about Gloria Tempest, about Daphne Croft, about Manelli. I told him about the book—all of it. He sat listening, chewing on his lower lip.

When I'd finished, he let out a heavy sigh. "A book, huh? You don't know what's in it?"

"I haven't any Idea. But whatever it is, Manelli wants it bad enough to go out looking for it himself at Shady Lodge. I figure it's important trouble for him if the wrong party picks it up."

"You think he killed Stevens and the girl to get it back?"

I settled into the seat. "Blackmail is always a good motive for murder."

"And this book might hang him?"

"Could be," I said. "But he won't just sit still and wait to take the big fall. And that puts Lenore Stevens in real danger. If her husband didn't have the book when he was killed, then he would have left it with someone close to him. With Stevens and his girlfriend both dead, Manelli has to figure the wife is his next stop."

Wells pushed his hat back and whistled through his teeth. "Son of a bitch. You're probably right. I'll get someone else out to the house." A knowing concern crept into his eyes. He looked over at me. "What are you going to do?"

I looked out into what was left of the rotten afternoon. I was cultivating a headache, and my ribs were still sore. I thought about my stomach. "I think I'll get something to eat."

Wells cracked his smile again. "You're a hard case, Garrett."

I got out of the car and went over and got into the DeSoto. Wells drove away. I bought myself a drink from the glove compartment. It made my insides feel like sandpaper. I burned up a couple of cigarettes and just sat. I looked back over at the Municipal Building. It was dark. This was a dark town. I thought about Ed Rawls again. I still didn't know what to tell him. Three people dead. Lenore Stevens might be next. And all I had were loose ends. Nice going, Garrett.

I started the car and drove back to the hotel, and went across the street to the cafeteria. I chewed on some kind of sandwich and thought about going back to see Lenore Stevens. While I was trying not to finish my sandwich, a kid in a wool cap and pea jacket rode his bicycle up to the front door. He leaned the bike against the building and stood in the doorway, trying to stay dry. I left the rest of the sandwich and went out and stood next to him.

"You deliver the papers?" I asked him.

He frowned at me through a few hundred freckles. "Hey, Mac." He pointed at his bike and the gray canvas bag in the basket. "What does that look like, a fruit salad?"

"Were you out here last night?"

He shoved his hands into the pockets of the pea jacket. "I'm out here every night."

"See anybody go into the hotel over there?"

His eyes narrowed, and he cocked his head to one side. "You a copper?"

"Not exactly."

"On a hustle, huh?" He leaned against the door and smiled. "What's it worth?"

I pulled out a buck, folded it in half lengthwise, and stretched it out in front of him. He took it and put it in his pocket.

"Yeah," he said. "Like I told the coppers, there was this dame. She come

CHAPTER THIRTEEN

around the corner and went into the hotel. She walked real quick, and she had her collar up, like maybe she didn't want to be spotted. She the one that got bumped?"

"Relax, kid. It's my dollar. Did you see anybody else? Maybe a big guy with dark red hair?"

"Naw. There was nobody else. Who goes out in this weather? I just finished folding and did my route."

I thanked him, gave him another dollar, and went across the street to the hotel. The old woman was behind the counter. I said I needed an address and asked for the city directory. She exhaled all over me and mumbled, "You Garrett?"

I groped through the gin fog and said I was Garrett.

"Guy's been callin' for you every five minutes since I don't know how long. Pain in the ass. Name's Solomon. Here's the number."

She stretched out a damp shaky hand and gave me a wadded-up slip of paper. I held my breath long enough to get across the lobby to the pay phone and put in my nickel. Solomon's voice was jumpy.

"I've been calling, and you're not answering," he said.

"What can I do for you, Mr. Solomon?"

"Something is going on. Can you come?"

"What is it?"

"On the phone, I'm not talking. Can you come? Right away?"

I told him I would and hung up. It took me ten minutes to get to the tailor shop. I circled the block behind it and gave the place the once-over. I wasn't sure what I was looking for, but I felt like looking anyway. I didn't see anything suspicious, so I pulled up by the front door and looked at it. Something told me I should have company. I took the .38 out of the glove compartment and tucked it in my belt. Then I got out, walked up to the entryway, and peered through the glass door. There were no lights on. The place looked empty. I tried the door. It was open.

I stepped inside, making as little noise as I could, and shut the door. I stood there with my back to it for a minute, listening to the darkened shop. There was no sound but the rain beating on the front steps and slapping against the window. I walked over by the counter. There was a careless pile of clothes in the middle of it. Men's suits. Expensive. The ones I'd seen yesterday. Next to the pile was a stub of chalk.

I moved around behind the counter and almost tripped over a pair of shoes. They were side by side on the floor, pointing at the ceiling. A man's feet were in the shoes. Solomon was stretched out on the floor behind the counter on his back, arms at his sides. His face was covered with welts and bruises, and a gash in his forehead was still leaking blood. It was running down his face and neck, staining his shirt and soaking into the tape measure that still hung around his neck. His nose was bluish, the lower half bent into a grotesque angle from the impact of a massive fist.

"Oh no," I said out loud. I bent over him and reached toward his neck to feel for a pulse. Only I felt something else. It was pressing between my shoulder blades. It was round and hard, like the end of a broom handle, or a very large gun.

"Don't move, flatfoot."

Chapter Fourteen

"Put your hands on the counter, palms down, fingers spread."

The hard thing in my back shoved me forward, and I slapped both hands on the counter just to keep from falling. A hand as wide as a tennis racket reached around, patted my stomach, and found the .38. Then the hand lifted the gun out of my belt and tossed it out on the counter next to the pile of clothes.

"Okay, smart guy. Move over by the window, nice and slow."

I did as I was told. Then I turned back and stood looking at Frankie Bell.

He was standing there, a sneering red-haired ape. He was wearing the same dungarees, plaid shirt, and leather jacket—and an automatic in his right hand. It was a .45, a big gun. In his hand, it looked like a toy. He grinned at me, an unfriendly grin.

"What took ya so long? I been tryin' to get ya here for over an hour."

"Saturday's my slow day," I said.

"Well, it ain't mine," he growled back.

"Yeah. I was at the Stevens's house. You've got real style, Frankie, beating up women and old men."

"Shut your goddamn mouth, Garrett."

He drew the gun back as if he might throw it at me. Then he brought it around and pointed it at me again.

"We're gonna have a talk," he went on. "Then, if there's anything left of you, I take you to the boss. He didn't say I had to leave you in one piece."

"The boss, huh? Is he going to pay me for finding Gloria Tempest?"

Bell let out a chuckle. "A real hotshot, ain't ya?" Then his face crowded into a snarl. "You know what he wants."

"Maybe he wants to give me your job. Maybe he thinks I can find his book without killing half the town."

I didn't think his face could get any uglier, but it did. "I ain't killed nobody!"

"No?" I had his attention now. "Well, it reads that you shot Stevens. You couldn't find the book at the motel or in his office, and the girl was out of sight. So, you put the tag on me. When she showed up in my room, you iced her. But she didn't have the book. So, you broke into the Stevens's house, making it look like a burglary." I watched his eyes jump. "You knew the house was being watched, didn't you?" There was the start of a smile, but he didn't speak. "The house wasn't very mussed up, not like Stevens's office. You must have known where to look." He stood there now, almost gloating. "Only you didn't find it, did you? You thought you had plenty of time, but Lenore Stevens surprised you, coming home early. Why didn't you shoot her too?" I slowly reached up and pushed my hat back on my head. "Not very tidy, Frankie, leaving her to finger you."

His voice became an angry whine. "You're full of crap. I don't shoot people." There was a twisted smile. "I break 'em."

"Maybe. But what about Ralph, the kid at the motel? He wasn't shot." I motioned toward the counter. "And what about him."

"Listen," he whined again. "I don't go to the lodge, ever. I was just there tailing you. And…" There was a groan and a stirring behind the counter. Bell's face eased into a grim satisfaction. "See? I don't kill people. I just make 'em wish they were dead. Like you're gonna."

"Okay, Frankie," I kept going. "Manelli's got you set up like a duck in a shooting gallery. Trying to hire me was just a cover. He put you out in the open. Think about it. The office, the house, tailing me. At least three people can identify you, maybe more. That book's a threat to him, so one by one, he knocks off the people who might have it. Only he stays undercover, and you go down for it." I watched a cloud of doubt cross his face. "What's in the book?"

He brought up his left hand and scratched his chin. "I don't know. I ain't never seen it."

CHAPTER FOURTEEN

There was a question in his eyes now, so I hammered on it. "He's playing you for a sucker, Frankie. Be smart. You might do some time, but you can let him take the big ride. Give me the gun."

He looked down at the gun, then back at me. I didn't have much left. I was fishing for my next line when Solomon bobbed up behind the counter like an old bald hand puppet. He looped the tape measure over the end of the .45 and jerked it hard. Bell lurched around toward the counter. It wasn't much, but it was enough.

I lunged at Bell and buried my fist in his stomach. The air whooshed out of him, and he doubled over, dropping the gun. There was no time to reach for it. I grabbed him by the shoulder and brought my knee up into the middle of his face. It was like kicking a watermelon. His brittle nose gave easily, jets of blood spurting from it, over my trousers and onto the floor. Instinctively, he brought his arms up over his face. I grabbed his jacket, and with all my strength, I ran him headfirst into the wall like a battering ram. His head hit the wall with a thud that shook the room, and he dropped to his knees.

I stood behind him and brought both fists down on the back of his neck. He buckled and put his right hand up over his head. But his left hand snaked out and caught my leg. He jerked me off-balance, and I pitched over, cracking the side of my head on the edge of the counter. I sprawled in front of it, dazed, feeling a warm trickle start down the side of my face. I tried to get up, but he was on me, his massive hands around my neck, squeezing tighter and tighter. I wanted to move my arms and legs, but I couldn't find them. The air began to slip away from me, and a red darkness was forming. Somewhere I heard a noise…thunk…thunk… Bell let go of me and reached up toward the counter. Soloman had picked up my .38 and was using the butt end of it on his head like a hammer. I shook my head clear while Bell put a hand in Solomon's face and pushed the old man back into the wall. I brought my foot up to Bell's chest, and with everything I had left, I kicked him back toward the front window.

He staggered backward and stopped. Somehow, he was on his feet, looming over me like King Kong. He wiped his face and looked at the blood on his hand. Then he leaned toward me with an angry grimace and raised two giant fists over my head.

I was finished, used up, just waiting for the crash and the darkness. I heard his voice. "Why you...."

The roar in the street blended with the tinkle of breaking glass. Bell hovered over me, the expression falling off his face. He dropped on top of me like a load off a gravel truck. I couldn't move. He was dead weight.

Solomon came around and tugged at Bell's legs enough for me to push him off and stand up. I leaned back against the counter and watched Sergeant Moran come into the shop waving his service revolver. He looked down at Bell, gave me a cold stare, and glanced over at Solomon. Then he slowly exhaled, tucked his gun under his coat, and looked back at me.

"Haven't you learned not to tangle with him, hotshot?"

I looked down at the lifeless heap on the floor in front of me. "Now I have."

Moran asked Solomon about a phone, and the old man took him into the back room. I picked up the .38 and tucked it back in my belt, and just leaned against the counter, trying to remember how to breathe. Moran made his call to the station and then came back and stood next to me, looking down at Bell.

"This ought to wrap things up," he said. Then he looked up at me. "You sure are lucky."

I stood there feeling every inch of my body. Even my hair hurt. I felt the cut on the side of my head. I looked down at the blood on my trench coat and trousers. Then I looked back at Moran. "Yeah. Don't I look it?"

Chapter Fifteen

"Garrett, I'm getting tired of this." Wells stood in the doorway of the tailor shop, bristling like a cat caught in a shower. "Every time I run into you, I have to scrape up a body."

I wanted to say something to him, but the words wouldn't come out. I just stood by the window and looked out at the coroner's crew wrestling Bell's draped body into the town ambulance. It took four of them. Another attendant was escorting Solomon out the door, but the old man stopped him and grabbed my arm. His face was covered with gauze and adhesive tape.

"Mr. Garrett, I wasn't really calling you. He made me do It. He wanted something, only he's not telling me what. He thinks maybe you leave something here in the shop. I'm telling him no. But he…he…"

"I know, Mr. Solomon. It's all right." I motioned toward the attendant. "You go with them now. They'll take care of you."

He nodded and began to move away. Then he stopped and looked at me again, a quiet triumph in his eyes. "It's like my Sophie said. You must stand up." He turned, and the two of them left.

Wells watched them go down the steps, then he spoke quietly to me. "Maybe you should go with them. Let the people at the hospital check you over." He hesitated. "You look terrible."

"Thanks," I said. "I'll bet you say that to all the girls."

He sighed and rolled his eyes toward the ceiling. "Rawls was right. Nobody gets through to you. Maybe I should just put you on a plane myself."

I pulled a mashed pack of cigarettes out of my coat, lit one, and took a deep drag. The smoke punished my lungs and chafed the back of my throat, and I stood there wondering why I was standing there. I looked back at Wells.

"Moran thinks it's all finished, that killing Bell closes your case."

"I know." He shrugged. "He told me. I don't buy it, but that's the way he sees it." A tired smile tried to climb up the sides of his face. "Did Bell say anything before you beat him up?"

"Very funny," I grunted. I leaned over and tossed the cigarette out the door and into the gutter before it killed me. "He said he didn't shoot anybody and that he'd never seen the book."

"You believe that?"

"It fits," I said. "Manelli wouldn't have trusted him with anything but street work. And Frankie wouldn't have gone to the trouble to make Stevens's death look like a suicide or to shoot Gloria Tempest with my gun. He wasn't that savvy."

Wells chuckled quietly. Then his face became serious. "You think this takes the heat off Lenore Stevens?"

I let out a slow, painful breath. "No. It's worse now. Bell could be recognized. Now we don't know who to look for. It's better than even money that Manelli still doesn't have the book and that he's getting desperate. If he thinks Stevens left the book with his wife, then she's in more danger than ever."

Wells shook his head slowly. He looked tired. "Yeah. I'll tell Moran to make sure she's covered." Then his eyebrows jumped up almost an inch, and he snapped his fingers. "Hey. I almost forgot. I called a friend of mine in Chicago and asked him to check on Mid-States Development. He called me back just before I came over here." His eyes brightened. He was in gear again. "They're mostly a paper company, probably set up as some kind of tax dodge. They seem to represent companies and wealthy individuals, people with money to invest who don't want to attract a lot of attention. And get this. My friend says that one of the controlling partners is Ray Floren, Mannie's old man. After that trial in Philly, he'd likely have it in for you."

The hair on the back of my neck stood at attention.

"Anyway," he went on, "Mid-States invests heavily in real estate and other financial institutions around the country. They put up some of the initial

CHAPTER FIFTEEN

capital when Stevens Associates was formed in 1946."

"So, when Stevens sold Wheelright to his own company, somebody else was really buying in."

He nodded. "Right. But there's more." I could see a glint in his eyes. He began reaching out with both hands, as if he was holding some found treasure. "Mid-States is a major investor in another Chicago financing firm, one that also has interests in this area."

I felt as if I'd just been handed a hot rivet. "Let me guess. Capital Investments Corporation?"

"Yeah." His face fell a foot, and his dark eyes began probing me. He went on slowly. "And they're represented by a Philadelphia law firm called…."

"Caulfield and Sanders," I drawled.

He dug both fists into his hips, and his eyes blazed at me. "Now, how the hell did you know that?"

"I eat a lot of fortune cookies."

"Look, Garrett…." A crimson flush rose on his face. He stood there with a frown that could have crawled all over me.

"Just guessing," I said. "Anything else?"

"No," he grumbled. "I'm not sure I'd give you anything more even if I had it. You're still holding out."

"Relax. I'll give you something you don't have. Bell knew the Stevens house was being watched."

The frown drifted away. "Are you sure? Did he say that?"

"No. But when I asked him about It, he looked like somebody caught hoarding food stamps." I shrugged. "He had to know."

Wells shook his head and gazed out the window. He spoke quietly to himself. "How could they? Not again. Not so soon. With Ralph, it took them six months."

"You got someone else at the lodge?"

He looked at me and ignored the question. "You can't be sure." His voice was hoarse, desperate.

I looked at him. "Can you?"

I left him standing there, wrapped in a look of disbelief that fitted him like a straitjacket.

I drove back to the hotel and made it all the way up to my room and into the bathroom. I stood there and leaned against the sink, holding onto it with both hands. The cold sweat came. It started at my temples and slid down my neck, across my back, and into my arms and legs. I stood there shivering. It was a familiar scene. I let it pass, then I looked up. The mirror still wasn't offering any charity. I washed the blood off my face and got as much of It off my clothes as I could. Then I changed my shirt and pulled a bandage out of my bag, and patched up the cut on my head.

I dragged myself out of the bathroom, sat on the bed, and thought. Maybe if I sat there long enough, it would come to me what I was doing here, in this town, on this case. I wasn't even sure what the case was. I had a client. I wasn't sure what I could do for her. She was in trouble. Now I was in trouble. I could just go back to L.A. People get killed there, too, only the climate is better. I could sit in my office and listen to my bills coming due. But I had a client, one that meant something to Ed Rawls.

I thought about the last two days. A dead man in a motel room, a dead girl in my bathroom, and a strangled motel clerk. I thought about Bell beating up Solomon, trying to beat up Lenore Stevens, and trying to turn me into tomorrow's headline. I thought about Manelli using me to find Gloria, using Bell to find his book, and using Daphne to find out what I knew. And I thought about two Chicago investment firms linked to Manelli and to Stevens. I looked at all the pieces one by one. I looked at them all together. They looked back. They were still just pieces.

I thought about how close Bell had come to killing me. I thought about how much of my life had been spent in cheap hotel rooms. And I thought about Lenore Stevens again. My head felt like the inside of a grapefruit. I stopped thinking.

I didn't have any first aid left in the nightstand, so I put my coat on and headed back downstairs, thinking of a dozen places I'd rather be. It was early evening when I got back into the DeSoto and headed north on Central.

Chapter Sixteen

The Country Club was one of those self-important places that seem proud of just being old. Behind a small but expensive stand of shrubbery, a three-story colonial mansion, white with black trim, looked out disdainfully on a pristine rolling lawn. At the edge of the lawn was a small wooden sign, painted white, with L.C.C. in black Gothic letters. A cobblestone drive curved off a street marked BOULEVARD drifted up toward the right of the mansion and emptied into a sprawling parking area. I cruised up into it and pulled the DeSoto in between a light gray Cadillac and a familiar green Hudson Hornet. I got out and headed up a flagstone walk to a narrow porch in front. It was covered by an arched roof extending out from the second story and held by two square white pillars. I tightened up the belt on my trench coat, walked up onto the porch, and pulled open a door as big as the entry to Fort Knox.

The long and narrow front hall was only the size of a subway station, and it was lined with arched doorways. It had a scalloped plaster ceiling, walls covered with a soft yellow paper textured like burlap, and a plush moss-colored carpet that dared you to walk on it hid the floor. I walked on it and looked around. That was as far as I got. A small dark efficient-looking man in a dark suit came through one of the doorways and announced himself as the club manager. I told him I wanted to see Mark Halstead. He made me feel as welcome as a toothache.

He ushered me through a doorway to the left and into a small square sitting room, then swiveled around and abruptly left. I took off my hat and looked around for a place to put it.

There was a heavily padded sofa and several chairs covered with a slate-blue corded fabric. Next to the sofa was a square end table. On it, a squat, antiseptic blue lamp with a stiff paper shade spread a harsh light around the room. In front of the sofa, a low coffee table held a display of magazines, carefully arranged like cards in a game of solitaire. I sat down on the sofa and put my hat on the table in front of me, and looked at the magazines. They were full of spring fashions and pictures of Tom Dewey making his run for President. Clearly, I was supposed to be impressed. I pulled out a crumpled cigarette, straightened it, and lit it just in time to see Mark Halstead make his entrance.

He was dressed as before, dark suit, creased trousers, and freshly laundered smile. He strolled over to me and held out his hand. "Oh yes," he said. "You're the one named Garrett."

I took his hand and nodded. He inspected me, working his way up from my shoes and stopping at the bandage on my head. "You look terrible," he said.

"No kidding?"

He settled into one of the chairs across from the sofa, crossed his legs, folded his hands, and tried to keep his smile from sliding off onto the floor.

"I don't see how I can help you," he said. "I've already told you and the police everything I know about the burglary."

"It isn't about the burglary," I told him.

He tightened his fingers just enough. "Oh?"

"I want to talk about Charles Stevens."

He lifted his hands in the air, still folded, and exhaled sharply. "Such a tragedy. He would have been a great man. He would have done important things."

"How important?"

He dropped his hands back in his lap and looked at me with genial disdain. "You must know how important Charles was to this town. He could have become just as important for the state." He leaned forward in the chair as if to say something only I should hear. "I do know why you're here, Mr. Garrett. Lenore told me about you."

CHAPTER SIXTEEN

"She didn't tell me about you. How long did you know Stevens?"

He inhaled this time. "I met Charles ten years ago in Philadelphia when he was arranging to buy the foundry. I represented him. Later he asked me to take over all his legal affairs. We became friends." He looked down toward his lap and shook his head. "Such a tragedy," he said again.

"So, you lined him up with Mid-States Development?"

He nodded slowly. The smile grew tentative. "It was simple financing. Mid-States invests money in growing businesses in return for part ownership. Charles needed capital to get started. It was a natural arrangement. My firm represented both parties."

"Convenient. What do you know about Capital Investments Corporation?"

"Nothing, really." His smile was hanging on by its fingernails. "But what can that have to do with Charles?"

"Probably nothing," I said. "Who takes over now that Stevens is dead?"

"That's rather complicated." He rearranged his hands in his lap, laying one over the other, and began drumming his Fingers. "Lenore is the only heir, of course. Charles never wanted children. She inherits all of Charles's estate… and his obligations. But Mid-States retains an operational partnership in Stevens Associates, which controls the foundry and the other holdings. So you see, it's not an ordinary inheritance. Lenore can try to take over for Charles, or she can appoint someone to act for her, although Mid-States must approve the appointee. She isn't likely to try it herself. Either way, she should stay pretty well fixed so long as she doesn't try to liquidate. If she does, Mid-States has the right of first refusal at a mutually agreeable price. Then it's hard to tell what would happen. They can be pretty hard-nosed."

"And where do you fit in?"

"Uh, naturally, I expect to be advising Lenore, looking out for her interests."

"Naturally."

His fingers stopped drumming. He began to look mildly annoyed. "As I said, we've been friends for a long time."

"You said you and Stevens were friends. How well do you know Mrs. Stevens?"

There was a quick flash in his eyes, like summer lightning. He held on to his smile, but it was growing cool, suspicious. "I don't understand your question."

"Never mind," I said. "I don't understand most of them myself. How well did Stevens and his wife get along?"

"Why, perfectly well, I should say. At least, if there was any trouble, I wasn't aware of it." He paused and looked pensive, as if I'd just given him the riddle of the ages. Then he pursed his lips and went on. "I do know the stories about Shady Lodge, so I suppose there must have been something wrong. But I didn't see it. In fact, we were expecting her to play a major role in his political career."

"Just one big happy family," I said. "Tell me about Stevens's politics."

He straightened in his chair and began speaking as if he were on the air.

"Charles was considering running for the Senate. A number of influential friends were trying to persuade him." He paused again and rubbed his chin. "I really don't know why he was hesitant."

"Maybe that's where Shady Lodge comes in."

"Perhaps." He nodded. "Still, it's too bad. He would have made a fine senator."

"With you helping him?"

His lips tightened. "I would have had a part in the campaign, of course."

"And now you've lost all that. Too bad. But I'm sure you can latch on to Mrs. Stevens for a meal ticket."

His smile did a half-gainer down his face. "Mr. Garrett, you're impertinent."

"Yeah," I said. "You're right. All my friends tell me that. And you're just the Good Samaritan lawyer looking after the family. You'll probably even give up your practice back in Philadelphia so you can devote yourself to looking after Lenore Stevens and her money. You're a smooth article, Halstead. But maybe you can explain to me why a Chicago investment firm like Mid-States would want a lawyer from back east who spends so much of his time here in Lancaster representing someone else?"

He didn't say anything, so I let him have both barrels. "Was Manelli one of the influential friends encouraging Stevens to go into politics?"

CHAPTER SIXTEEN

His jaw set, and his eyes glistened with the warmth of dry Ice. He seemed ready to say something, but the small dark man minced in and handed him a piece of paper. Halstead read the note and stood up. His smile came back in place, and his voice had a sneer in it.

"Mr. Garrett, you are simply a cheap little man. Men like you are bought and sold every day. And to me, you are an item of no consequence. I have indulged you this far out of consideration for Lenore. But now I can see that further discussion with you is pointless, and I must attend to other matters. I'm sure you'll understand that I don't wish to see you again." He turned and walked out.

I left the club and went out and sat in the car. He was a smooth article, all right. Just a friend of the family, looking out for everybody's best interests, taking nothing for himself.

I pulled out and headed the car down the drive and into the street. Across from the entrance, several stately houses were showing off some dormant but expensive landscaping, and wondering what I was doing in their neighborhood. I cruised about a hundred feet up the Boulevard and turned onto a side street. I swung around and pulled up to the corner where I could see the entrance to the country club. Then I cut the motor, turned off the lights, and waited.

An oppressive mist covered the windshield, making it hard to see. I rolled down the driver's window and sat there. The withering cold seeped into my bones. I could still feel Frankie Bell's giant hands on my neck. I started shivering again and reached for the glove compartment. But before I could get it open, the green Hudson came out of the country club entrance, turned left, and headed past me on its way toward town. I started the DeSoto and listened to its coughing protest as I pulled out and started off in the same direction.

The Hudson seemed to make every light as it wound down to Central, turned left again, sailed through Lancaster's business district, and then pulled up in front of Ryan's Tavern. I'd lost sight of it twice, but I cheated on enough lights to keep up, the DeSoto struggling all the way. I drove a block past Ryan's, turned the corner, and left the car out of sight. The cold mist stung my face as I slipped out of the car, ran over to the corner, and peered around the side of an old brown rowhouse.

I was just in time to see Halstead in the dim light coming from the pub. He wore a dark gray hat and a trench coat like mine, only he left the wrinkles home. In his right hand, he was carrying a brown leather briefcase that bounced against his leg as he walked. It looked heavy. He opened the front door, gingerly eased the bag in ahead of him, and followed it inside.

Sometimes I like to reflect. I lit a cigarette and thought about what a great life doing detective work is. You get to visit interesting places. You get to meet interesting people. It's all anybody could ask for. Just don't think about tomorrow, or about a lot of meaningless yesterdays. They blur. They become all the same. Only the ugliness stays with you.

I was busy feeling as good as a nickel shave when Halstead came out of Ryan's and bounded across the street to his car, moving like Jesse Owens with a hotfoot. The hat was in place. The coat hadn't picked up any wrinkles. In fact, he hadn't picked up anything. But he had left something. He wasn't carrying the briefcase.

The Hudson did a U-turn in the street and headed back up Central. I listened as the tires swished away and grew faint. Then they were gone. I looked up and down the street. It was dark, quiet. Nothing moved. I looked over at Ryan's. A grayish light was coming out of the windows, making the mist outside look almost like smoke. The smart thing to do was to go back to the hotel and forget the whole thing. Instead, I started across the street.

Chapter Seventeen

The inside of Ryan's gave me that empty feeling you get at funerals. Two yellowish overhead lamps dropped just enough light to show the empty tables and booths and the scattered particles of nestling dust. I stepped in and pushed the door closed behind me, taking in the stifling smell of stale beer. There were no customers, the tables were cleaned off, and a stack of cloudy-looking glasses stood precariously near the end of the bar. Beyond the glasses, the same round, red-faced bartender that I'd seen two days ago stood perched over the bar on his elbows with a newspaper spread out in front of him.

As I came in, he looked up at me with the same interest an old dowager might show a panhandler. He was wearing dark trousers and a white shirt, with the collar open and the sleeves rolled partway up over his short, meaty arms. He was something less than six feet tall and built like an overweight fire hydrant. A patch of short brown hair, streaked with white, covered his head and jutted out like an awning over a fleshy, weathered face. His gray-brown eyes had the same cloudy expression as the glasses on the bar. It was a face that had been through a lot of hard nights in what must have been more than fifty years.

I moved toward him, and he stuck his nose back down into the classifieds. I sat down on the stool in front of him. He didn't move. I took off my hat and dropped it in the middle of the paper. He moved.

"Hey, watch it, will ya, bud?" He stood up, his hands still resting on the edge of the bar, his face an irritated red. "What the hell do you think this is?"

"Lost and found?"

His irritation slipped into impatience. "Beat it, will ya? We're closed."

"I'm not interested in keeping you open," I said. "I'm just here to meet someone, a man named Mark Halstead."

He folded his arms across his chest and pushed his jaw out at me. "Look, bud. Nobody's been in here. Why would they on a night like this? So how 'bout just running along?"

"Wrong answer," I said. "Let's try again. His name is Mark Halstead. He's about my height, dark hair, and features, good-looking. He'd be dressed the same way I am, in a hat and trench coat."

The man's face hardened, the red in it showing a hint of purple. "Look. I told ya. Nobody's been in here. Now drift. Don't make me get tough."

"Don't be silly," I said. "I've got height and reach on you. I've got you by ten, maybe fifteen years. And I fight dirty." I opened my coat just enough to let him see the butt of the .38 sticking up over my belt.

His hands fell helplessly back to the bar, the corners of his mouth following them down. "All right, all right. Gimme a break, will ya, bud?" He looked down and shuffled his feet, then looked up again, his breathing shortened. "There was a guy, like you said. Only he didn't look like you. He was...." He hesitated, his eyes drifting over the front of my trench coat. "He was neater."

I decided not to trade wisecracks. "So, he was here. And he left something for me?"

He stiffened. "No." His eyes fluttered down toward my belt. "I mean... Look, mister. I don't know the guy. He just comes in here every month or so, has a beer, and leaves."

"Sure," I said. "You're just running a nice quiet place. No fuss." I leaned across the bar toward him. "Where's the case?"

He brought his jaw up and sucked in on his lower lip, somehow missing the end of his nose. He began blinking hard and fast. "Please, mister. Lay off, will ya?" His voice held a twitter that sounded like a frightened canary. "Frankie...Frankie Bell. He's due in here any minute. If I don't give it to him, I'm cold meat."

"Frankie's had a slight change of plans." I leaned back on the stool, giving him another look at the .38. "He won't be coming in anymore."

CHAPTER SEVENTEEN

His mouth fell open, and his eyes widened enough to reach the ceiling. He just stood there for a minute. Then his voice seemed to come in out of the rain, cold and shaking. "Frankie? You?"

A gentle push would have knocked him over. I pushed. "The case?"

He moved like a cat that had just stepped on a hot stove. He ducked down behind the bar and brought up the briefcase, and dropped it in front of me as if it burned his hands. Then he stepped back and nervously shifted his weight from foot to foot.

I took it by the handle and put it on the stool next to me. Then I looked up at him again. "Has Halstead left this for Frankie before?"

He nodded rapidly, the pouches under his eyes bobbing like wet teabags over a hot cup. "Sure. Every month he comes in here. He drops the bag, picks up the envelope, and leaves. Then Frankie comes in…." He stopped and swallowed. "Ya see, Frankie always comes in an hour before this Halstead guy gets here and gives me the envelope. Only tonight, Frankie doesn't show." He stopped abruptly, the muscles in his neck tensing.

"Uh-huh."

His eyes went to my belt again. Then he put both hands on the bar and leaned toward me. "Listen." He spoke in a hoarse whisper. "I don't know nothin'. I don't want to know nothin'. You guys come in, leave things, pick up things. I just wanna stay outta the way."

I didn't say anything. He brought his hands up and rubbed the palms together, leaving a pair of moist spots on the edge of the bar.

"Look," he said, "this Halstead. He didn't like it that I had no envelope for him. I tried to tell him I don't know nothin', but he was real mad. He even wrote something and left it in there." He nodded toward the bag. Then he pushed a sweaty palm toward me. "You tell him, will ya, bud? Tell him I don't know nothin'."

I put both elbows on the bar, leaned forward, and brought my voice up at him out of my shoes. "What's your name?"

He put his hands back together, and the red began rising in his face again. "Marty."

"Okay, Marty. I'll tell him. You don't know nothin'." I grabbed the briefcase and stood up. "You know enough to bring me a beer?"

"Sure. Sure." He scampered off toward the end of the bar. I went over to the booth in the corner and sat down. Marty brought the beer and then hustled back behind the bar. He grabbed a rag and made himself as busy as an alderman on election day. He didn't know nothin'.

I sipped the beer and started to miss the Old Kentucky. I put the briefcase on my lap, unbuckled the flap, and pulled the top open. The money was there, fifties and hundreds, stacked and taped into neat bundles. Each bundle had to be a grand. There was enough to buy a house in the country, with a golf course, pool, and tennis court. No wonder Halstead had to struggle. It's not easy carrying thirty pounds of money.

On top of the money, folded lengthwise, was a sheet of paper with two columns of typed figures. I stared at them for a minute. They could have been dates. They could have been amounts. They could have been anything. I folded the paper and put it back, and fingered around the piles.

Halstead's note was shoved down on the side. I pulled it out, opened it, and read it: "Must have monthly accounting. Noon tomorrow." I stuffed the note back inside and put the bag down on the seat next to me. Then I just sipped the beer and waited.

I sat there, sipping and waiting and watching Marty polish everything but his shoes. The beer was almost gone when a man came in through the front door. He was a big man, moving slowly, deliberately. It was Sergeant Moran. He ambled up to the bar, exchanged a quick word with Marty, then turned and looked over at me. He walked slowly over to the booth and sat down across from me, taking his hat off and shaking the rain from it onto the floor. He put the hat on the seat next to him and folded his hands, and looked at me.

"Garrett, you just keep showing up everywhere in town."

"In this town, it's easy," I said. I watched him sit there. He started to rub his hands as if to get them warm. "I thought you were out at the Stevens house."

He shook his head. "I was, only I'm off duty now. Ferris is out there."

Marty trotted over with another beer and put it down in front of Moran. Then he scuttled off, and Moran lifted the glass and drained it. He clinked

CHAPTER SEVENTEEN

the empty glass down on the table and wiped the back of his hand across his mouth.

"By the way," he said, "that Stevens dame wants to see you. She said if I ran into you, I should let you know."

"What does she want?"

"She didn't say."

I felt like biting off the end of the table. "Is that why you're here, or are you still tagging after me for Wells?"

He brought up his hand again and rubbed the right side of his neck. "Naw. The lieutenant says to lay off you, so we lay off."

"Then what are you doing here?"

"Me? I live here." He shrugged. "Or at least near here. I live in the brown rowhouse across the street. I always come in for a cold one after work." He read the disappointment on my face. "Look. I already saved your bacon once today. That's enough." His eyes fell on the briefcase next to me. "What's with the bag? You leaving town?"

I let my breath out heavily. "No jokes tonight, Moran. I'm not in the mood." I finished the rest of the beer and pushed the glass to one side. "It's a bundle left here for Manelli. Frankie Bell was supposed to pick It up."

"What's in it?"

"A heavy stash, a bagful, probably from out of town."

"Jesus," he breathed. "The whole bag?"

I just nodded.

He put both hands flat on the table and stared at the briefcase. "You think it's hot?"

"Hot enough to burn from here to Chicago."

"Jesus." He lifted a hand and rubbed his neck again. Then finally, he looked over at me. "What do we do?"

I lit a cigarette and let the smoke out slowly. It tasted as stale as the beer. "By now, Manelli must know that Bell is dead. He'll have to send someone else after the money. It might be the same party that would show up at the Stevens house. I was waiting here to see who that would be. But then you walked in."

I stubbed out the cigarette in a small tin ashtray in the corner of the booth. "I'll have to go out and see Mrs. Stevens. Can you stay here?"

"Sure."

"Give the bag back to Marty, and tell him to flash you a signal when the pickup is made. Then go across the street. Don't wait in here. When you see the guy take the bag, call Wells and tell him."

"Okay." He started to frown. "But why don't I just put the arm on the guy?"

"Because he's not the one we want. He'll only be a soldier."

The frown eased. "So, I follow him?"

"You won't have to. He'll be taking the bag to Manelli."

"Suppose he don't show?"

"Then take the bag to Wells."

"Okay," he grunted.

Moran folded his hands on the table again and let his eyebrows droop downward. "Garrett," he said," I think I owe you an apology. I had you figured for rubbing that dame, and maybe the Stevens guy. But the lieutenant told me what you've been doing. He told me how Manelli set you up at the hotel last night. And he told me why Bell was at the Stevens house and at the tailor shop. I guess I had you wrong." He paused, waiting for me to respond. I didn't.

He rubbed his neck some more. "Anyway, I'm sorry we rousted you."

"Forget it."

I left him sitting there, and I went outside feeling as if something was crawling on me. As I walked to the car, my arms and legs ached. I got in and tossed the .38 into the glove compartment. Then I pulled back onto Central and headed out to the Stevens house. You don't get many apologies in my trade. You don't expect many.

Chapter Eighteen

Almost as soon as I knocked, Lenore Stevens opened the door. A filmy white kerchief hung loosely around her neck as if she'd just pushed it back off her hair. She wore a tan, belted trench coat that was still wet from the evening. And she wasn't wearing shoes.

"Oh. It's you," she said. "I've been out taking Rogers and Martha to town. They have Sundays off, and they both have relatives in Philadelphia. So I drove them to the station."

She moved back, and I stepped into the entrance hall and shut the door. "You wanted to see me?"

"Yes. I told Sergeant Moran…."

She stopped and stared at the bandage on my head. Then her stare slowly moved down over my coat and trousers. Finally, she looked up.

"Oh my," she said. "You look terrible."

"Thanks," I said. "You're about the fourth person who's told me that today."

She looked me over again, then quickly brought her hand up over her mouth. She chuckled. "Oh, dear." She chuckled again and shook her head. She started to laugh. "I'm sorry. But it's funny. Look at you. My noble detective." She brought her hands together, put her head back, and let out a real burst of laughter.

I stood there, ready to throw her out the window. I might have, if I hadn't done something else instead. I kissed her, quickly, firmly, holding her arms against her sides. She drew back and looked at me, wide-eyed, startled. I kissed her again, this time slowly, deliberately. I slid my hand around to the small of her back, drawing her up against me. She responded. We stood locked together, breathing Into each other, drifting away from the ugliness of the last two days. Finally, we separated, and she looked up at me, her brown eyes moist and deep.

"Well." Her voice was husky. She adjusted her clothes the way women do at such moments. Then a trace of playfulness darted across her expression. "Mr. Garrett, do you provide that service for all your clients?"

"Only the young pretty ones," I said. "And only on cold, wet nights, after someone has just died all over my best suit."

"What?" She put her hands up to her face, her eyes widening.

"Don't feel too badly," I said. "You won't find Frankie Bell in your closet anymore."

She reached up and lightly touched the bandage on my head. "Is that how you got this?"

I nodded. "Bell and I had a minor disagreement."

"How awful. Please come in and sit down." She put her hand on my arm. "I'm sure you could use a drink."

I took off my coat and hat and piled them on the table by the tapestry. Under the table was a pair of black high-heeled shoes. They were wet and streaked with mud. Before I could say anything, she reached down and picked them up.

"What a dreadful night," she said. "Poor Martha is getting old, and she doesn't walk too well when it's slippery. I had to help her into the station. As we were crossing the street, a large black car raced right past. It almost hit us. As it was, we were both soaked." She held up the shoes. "I'm afraid they're ruined."

I felt as if someone had just poured icy water down my back. "Be thankful you only got wet."

"What do you mean?"

I sighed heavily and dodged the question. "You said something about a drink?"

She led me to the back of the house and into the kitchen. She peeled off her trench coat and draped it over a chair, then went over to a cupboard by the sink. She was wearing a narrow tan skirt and a soft brown sweater that

CHAPTER EIGHTEEN

buttoned up the front. It gave her almost enough room to breathe. As she reached up into the cupboard, the sweater rode up on her side, exposing a firm, silky stretch of midriff. She brought out a couple of tall glasses, turned, and looked at me looking at her. She smiled and pulled the sweater back in place. Then she handed me the glasses, picked up a smoky-colored decanter from the counter, and motioned to her right. "This way."

We went into a sitting room off the kitchen. It was small and dark, the only light coming from several quietly burning logs in a stone fireplace on the left. In the middle of the pegged oak floor was an oval chocolate-colored rug holding a rustic coffee table styled like an old cobbler's bench. Against the wall to the right facing the fireplace was a high-backed, Colonial-style sofa with brown and white floral-print upholstery. Beyond the sofa in the corner was an ornate brass floor lamp. And across from it was a Boston rocker. It was a warm room, maybe the warmest place in town.

I put the glasses down on the table next to several stacks of papers, folders, and notebooks. Lenore poured several fingers from the decanter into one of the glasses and handed it to me. "You look like a Scotch drinker. And no ice. Am I right?"

"Close enough."

I took the glass and walked over by the fireplace. I sipped the Scotch and studied the solitary picture on the mantelpiece. It showed Lenore and her husband standing on a sidewalk in front of a cafe, arms around each other. They looked very young and innocent. It must have been an old picture.

She came up behind me and spoke quietly. "That was taken in Philadelphia just before we were married." She sighed deeply. "Things were very… different then." She pursed her lips. "Charles was a very private person in his way. That's the only picture I have of the two of us."

Something about the picture made it hard for me to stop looking at it. But she put her hand on my arm, and I turned toward her. She reached up and brushed the tips of her fingers over my forehead and past the bandage.

"Does it hurt?" she asked.

"Everything hurts."

"Tell me what happened."

I emptied my glass and set it on the mantel. She looked at me, composed, waiting.

"Bell suckered me to a tailor shop by beating up an old man who made the mistake of talking to me. After he beat up the tailor, he tried to take me apart." I glanced down at the bloodstains on my trousers. "I guess I wasn't so easy. I held him off long enough for Sergeant Moran to come and gun him down."

She shuddered. "You make it sound so cold, so matter-of-fact."

"You get that way in this business."

"But you were in danger."

"That's part of it," I said. "Anyway, you won't have to worry about Bell."

She leaned forward and put her hand on my cheek. "My noble detective." she gazed up at me, her brown eyes inviting me to dive in. "There's something else, isn't there? Something about that car tonight?"

"You shouldn't have gone out. You were safe here with the police watching."

"But I thought that Bell person...."

I grabbed both her arms above the elbow. "It isn't him. It's Manelli. He's desperate. He's been looking for a book that your husband and Gloria Tempest stole from him. After the girl was rubbed out, her apartment was searched, probably by a cute little trick named Daphne, who lives across the hall. She just happens to work at the Silver Club. But she didn't find the book. That's why Frankie Bell was out here today. You crossed him up by coming home when you did. Then somehow, Manelli got the idea that I might have the book. So, he had Bell lean on the tailor in order to get to me."

I saw her wince, and I realized how hard I was squeezing her arms. I pried my hands loose and let them drop.

"Manelli's still looking for that book, and everyone who might have it and use it against him is turning up dead."

She tensed. "Then you think it was Manelli in the car? That he was trying to kill me?"

"I don't know. Maybe it was just coincidence. But it's not worth taking the risk." I searched her eyes. There was fear. But there was also strength, the deep-down kind that you only see when the chips are down. I figured they

CHAPTER EIGHTEEN

were. "Do you have a gun in the house?"

She swallowed slowly. "Yes. Charles had a pair of matching pistols. He kept one in his office. The other one is upstairs."

"Keep it with you," I said. "Manelli isn't going to stop just because Frankie Bell is dead."

She put her arms tight around me and pressed the side of her face into my chest. "That awful man. I wish the world could be rid of him."

I put my arms around her. "Then you wouldn't need me."

She looked up at me, her face just inches from mine, and whispered, "Wouldn't I?"

This time she kissed me, a lingering kiss, the kind that tells you there's plenty of time. We took in the warmth from the fireplace, and from each other. When we separated, she put her head against my chest again and breathed contentedly.

"What have I gotten you into? Poor Mr...." She brought her head back abruptly and looked at me, an impish grin playing around the pout of her lower lip. "Under the circumstances, I can't very well keep calling you Mr. Garrett, can I?"

"I suppose not."

She brought her hands around and rested them on the front of my chest. "Is Michael all right?"

"Fine," I said. I took her hands off my chest and held them together in front of her. "But this will keep. Why did you want to see me?"

She moved away from me and motioned toward the coffee table. "I've been going through my husband's things, his personal papers. I didn't find any book like the one you described. But I thought you might want to look for yourself."

I went over and sat on the sofa. Lenore settled down beside me with her feet tucked up next to her. The sweater and skirt were stretched tight across the curve of her flank. I swallowed hard and began thumbing through the piles of paper. There wasn't much to find, bank statements, canceled checks, a few letters. But nothing about Stevens or his business that I didn't already know.

I leaned back into the sofa and looked at Lenore. "What happens to the business now that your husband isn't around?"

She sighed. "I don't know. Mark has offered to fill in and run things temporarily, until I can find someone else or until I can arrange a settlement with Charles's partners." She shook her head. "It's all so complicated." She looked over at me. "I don't even know who his partners are."

"How will you live?"

"I have some money," she said. "I'm not rich, but I have enough to get by." She turned and stared into the fireplace. "I'll have to sell the house, of course. And I'll have to let Rogers and Martha go. But in a way, it will be a relief." She squeezed her eyes shut, then blinked them open as if to sweep away some painful memory. "I never wanted all this. Charles just never understood."

"Was Halstead pushing him to run for office?"

"Why, yes." She looked over at me again. "Mark represents a number of important people. He said he could get them to back Charles and that Charles would make a wonderful senator."

"Only Charles wouldn't go for it?"

She bit her lip. "I'm afraid that was my fault. I didn't want him to run. I was still hoping that somehow we could make our marriage work. I knew that if Charles went into politics, he'd have to be away a lot, and there would be…temptations. We just wouldn't have a chance. So, I told him he'd have to choose between his politics and our marriage." She squeezed her hands together. "I suppose it was selfish of me, and Charles reacted badly." Her mouth set in a grim smile. "A broken marriage is poison for a political career. So then Charles stopped having anything to do with me. He would simply stay away for days at a time. I guess he was with that…woman."

"How did you first meet Charles?"

She exhaled heavily and leaned her head back against the cushions. It was at a café in Philadelphia, the one in the picture." She motioned toward the mantel. "I was there with Edward. Charles saw me and insisted on dancing with me. He simply wouldn't leave us alone until I told him my name. Then for days, he just kept after me. He called all the time and sent me flowers every day." She smiled softly, a distant sparkle showing in her eyes. "He was

CHAPTER EIGHTEEN

so romantic." Then the sparkle faded. She sighed a long sigh. "But that was a long time ago."

I rubbed my hands together, just to be doing something with them. "I guess that's when Ed Rawls went to LA."

"Yes," she sighed. "Poor Edward. I'm sure he wanted me to be more than just a friend. But I couldn't." She chewed on her lip again. "If I'd only known. Charles became so ambitious, so wrapped up in his business. I was like one of his possessions, all for the sake of appearances." She put her hand on my shoulder. "I've often wondered what it would be like not having to pretend, and to be with someone who didn't care what people thought about him."

I moved her hand off my shoulder. "You wouldn't like it."

"How do you know?" The playful smile returned. "With someone like you…."

"With someone like me, you'd wind up in a one-room walk-up, with nothing but cold coffee and a sink full of dirty socks."

She chuckled. "Such a tough guy. I think I'd love every minute of it."

I got up and went over to the fireplace. She moved over and stood next to me. The glow from the embers flickered in her eyes. "Michael, what's the matter?" she asked.

I was about to tell her when the phone rang in the kitchen. She went out to answer it, and I stood there studying the picture on the mantel. I heard her pick up the phone.

"Hello… Oh. Yes, Lieutenant…. No. He left here some time ago…. Why yes, he's here. Just a minute." She came and stood in the doorway and looked in at me. "It's for you. It's Lieutenant Wells."

I went into the kitchen and picked up the receiver off the counter. "Garrett."

"Garrett, have you seen Moran? He was supposed to check in when he got off duty, and I haven't heard from him."

"Yeah," I said. "I saw him about an hour ago at Ryan's. He's going to be busy for a while."

"What?"

"Are you in your office?"

"Yeah, but…."

"I'll tell you about it when I see you."

"Garrett," he hollered.

"Stay there." I hung up.

Lenore was standing beside me. I turned and looked at her. "I have to leave. Manelli may still be looking for me. I want to find him first."

"Be careful, Michael." She put her arms around my neck and molded her body to me like a warm bath. She rested her head against my shoulder and murmured into my neck. "I wish you could stay."

I wanted to stay. That's why I left.

The night had dried up and gotten even colder. The wind roared at me out of the darkness. It pushed against me like a bouncer at a dime-a-dance joint, as if to keep me away from something. I let the DeSoto drive itself back to town while I sat and muddled things over with what was left of my brain. My thoughts nagged at me out of their own shadows. They taunted me about something forgotten, something from the past, something at the hotel. I thought about seeing Wells. But not right away.

I pulled up in front of the hotel and got out of the car. As I trudged up to the door, a gust of wind almost took me into the next block. I ducked inside and shut the door, and started toward the stairs. Then I saw her.

"Mr. Garrett."

She climbed up off the old red couch and stumbled across the lobby in my direction. It took her a while. She was reeling drunk.

Chapter Nineteen

She lurched over to me, paused, and then pitched face-first against my chest. I caught her under the shoulders, hoisted her up, and held her at arm's length. Her breath surrounded me with whiskey. She was wearing a forgettable blue coat, no glasses, and a look from the bottom of the barrel. It was like seeing a character in a cartoon. I was looking into the bleary-eyed face of Winnie Adams.

"Winnie, what are you doing here?"

Her voice gurgled like water draining in a sump. "I came to find you…but you're gone…just like everything else. Everything's gone."

"What's gone?"

"The foundry, my job, my…." She wrinkled her face into something like a frown and cocked her head sideways over her shoulder. "Aren't you gone too?"

"I'm beginning to think so."

She began tottering, so I slipped an arm around her waist and aimed her at the couch.

"Let's sit down," I said.

I shoveled her onto the couch and sat down next to her, holding one of her arms to keep her propped up. Her eyes traveled around the lobby, not looking at anything in particular. I shook her, and she turned toward me.

"All right, Winnie, tell me what's going on."

She brought her words out and let them fall slowly, quietly, like the steps of a sleepwalker. "They're closing the foundry."

"Who is?"

"Mr. Halstead...he was in this morning. He said that...with Mr. Stevens gone, they might have to sell the foundry. He said I'd have to find another job."

"Who might have to sell?"

"I don't know."

She began to lean over sideways away from me. I tugged on her arm and jerked her upright.

"Winnie," I said, "this is Saturday. What were you doing in the office today?"

"I don't have any place else...to go." Her voice wandered off. She was drifting into an eighty-proof reverie. "It's so sad...Mr. Stevens is gone. Everybody's gone. Now...without my job, what will I do?" She sighed heavily and slumped against my shoulder. "His wife came this afternoon...to pick up some of his things. She said they were all she had to remember him. She wants his office locked up...just the way he left it, the way it was before...." She turned to me accusingly. "She even brought in a locksmith...to fix the drawer that you broke open." She poked a finger into my chest. "You weren't very nice, breaking into Mr. Stevens's desk."

I shrugged it off. "Did Halstead say anything else about selling the foundry?"

She opened her mouth to answer when a blast of loud music from a radio in one of the rooms rolled down the stairs and across the lobby. It was a strong blues number that brought her up as if an alarm clock had gone off. She stood up and weaved around a little and listened, "Oh, the music," she muttered. "Don't you love it?"

"Not tonight," I said.

She stood there, tottering for a minute. Then she put her hands together over her head and did a bump and grind that almost lifted me off the couch.

I stared at her. "Where did you learn that?"

"Oh, I just...learned it." She circled slowly, humming and moving invitingly with the music until she was facing me. Then she stopped and held out her arms. "Aren't you going to dance with me?"

"I'll dance with you from here."

She let her arms drop to her sides and attempted another frown. "You're teasing."

CHAPTER NINETEEN

"Me? Never."

She giggled and began floating toward me. "I like you," she slurred. "You're really smooze."

I nodded. "That's me alright, smooze."

She tumbled onto the couch and stared at me without actually seeing me. "Do you like me?"

I could see what was coming. "Look, Winnie," I said. "You're a nice girl. And I don't get to meet many. But I'm wearing shoes that are older than you are. Why don't I just take you home?"

For a minute, she just sat. Then her eyes turned glassy, and she pitched forward across my lap, out cold. I'm just great with sweet nothings.

I picked up a small brown purse that she had left on the floor, wedged under the front of the couch. There were the usual odds and ends. I found her glasses and a wallet with a driver's license. It listed "Winifred Adams, 241-B North Hamilton Place." I stretched her out on the couch and went over behind the front desk. I found a tattered city street directory and checked for the location on the driver's license. It was downtown, about a block from the Municipal Building.

I went back, pulled Winnie up off the couch, and wrapped her coat around her. She was as easy to handle as a sack of loose gravel. I hoisted her over my shoulder and lugged her out to the car.

Number 241-B North Hamilton Place was one side of a fading-white two-family house. It was part of a neighborhood that was being worn away by time and neglect. Two gnarled bare elm trees stood in the front yard, looming over the stubble of a hedge. A crumbling cement walk ushered the way up to a wood-slatted front porch with two doors and a blistered coat of dark green paint that was trying to hold on. There were no lights on in the house, and the only streetlamp was half a block away.

I pulled the DeSoto up to the curb across from the house, got out, and stood looking up and down the street, listening. The night was full of a stealthy quiet. I reached into the car and pulled the .38 out of the glove compartment. Then I hauled Winnie out of the front seat and up to the porch. She didn't object. At the door on the right, I fumbled through her purse and found a set of keys. The fourth one opened the door. I stumbled in, shut the door, and flipped on a wall switch.

A harsh overhead light showed an old green stuffed couch on the left and two upright wooden chairs. A faded umber throw rug was crumpled on the floor in front of the couch. In the corner by the door, a tarnished brass floor lamp was standing under a pleated paper shade with a shroud of cobwebs covering the top. To the right, an old console Victrola, nicked and scratched as if someone had gnawed on it, was sitting against the wall between two narrow windows covered with yellow-brown splotched shades. And around the room, a faded rose-pink wallpaper with rococo figures was cracked and peeling and giving the room a melancholic air.

At the back of the room, a short hallway led to the rear of the house and separated what I guessed would be a kitchen and a bedroom. I trudged across the room and through the doorway into the hall. I found the bedroom on the right. By now, Winnie was weighing on my shoulder like a duffel bag full of lead. I dropped her onto a metal frame bed that sat in the middle of a bare wood floor. Then I straightened up and rubbed my arm and shoulder while I looked around.

The room had all the comforts of a bus station. There was the bed, a plain wooden dresser with a mirror attached, and a nightstand like the one in my hotel. On the stand was a small lamp, a telephone, and a pile of wadded-up handkerchiefs. The walls were empty and covered by a cracked, bone-colored paint, and there was a door on the right. I opened it and found a closet with a string hanging down from a lone light bulb in a ceiling fixture. I pulled the string and looked at a wardrobe that could have outfitted the entire Ziegfeld Follies.

There must have been two dozen dresses, all the kind that would only be worn after dark. I checked the labels. Each one came from a store with a name that sounded like money. On the floor were more than a few pairs of high-heeled shoes, expensive and not made for much walking. There were two or three coats, full length, one trimmed with dark fur. And there were several unmatched suitcases piled in the corner. Along the left wall was

CHAPTER NINETEEN

a shelf with a blanket on it. I grabbed the blanket and went back into the bedroom.

Winnie was making raspish, throaty sounds and rolling her head from side to side. I unfastened her coat and propped her up, and began slipping it off. Her eyes bobbed open, showing the clear brilliance of a dirty windshield. She flopped a limp arm over my shoulder and began whimpering into my shirt. "Please don't go. Don't leave me here alone. I won't be any trouble. Take me with you. Please."

I dragged her coat off and stretched her out again, and spread the blanket over her. Her head fell over to the side, and her breathing tumbled out, ragged and harsh. I listened for a minute. The breathing continued.

On the dresser, I spotted a bottle of Old Kentucky, about half full. I picked up the bottle and helped myself. I walked back out into the living room, went over to the door, and shut off the light. I stood there for a minute, looking back, wondering. The breathing sounds from the bedroom persisted. I ducked out the door and headed down the walk.

Chapter Twenty

As I started into the street, a black Buick Roadmaster sedan came around the corner and growled up in front of me, and sat there idling in a smooth expensive purr. It had white sidewalls, a few hundred pounds of chrome, and a midnight-luster finish. Before I could move, a couple of characters in dark coats and hats jumped out of the front seat and flanked me like muscle-bound bookends. One was tall, with a narrow stony face, mustard-colored skin, and a wide purple scar down his right cheek. The other had a round, pale, babyish face. He had bright blue eyes and a thin-lipped mouth set in a permanent sneer with a toothpick stuck in the side. They both looked at me as if I might be something they had lost and wanted back very much. I could guess why.

They were quick, practiced. The tall one shoved me against the front door while the other one reached inside my coat and took out the .38. I tried looking around, but a hand that felt like an anvil pounded into my back and flattened me against the side of the car. Then I heard a voice, low and smooth like the idling engine. "The boss wants to see ya, pal."

They opened the back door and tossed me inside like so much dirty laundry. The man with the scar climbed behind the wheel, put the Buick in gear, and headed slowly down the street. His playmate sat next to him, leaning back toward me, grinning and chewing on the toothpick. He brought up my .38, casually resting it on the back of the seat, and pointed it at my Adam's apple. I looked at the gun. I might as well have left it in the pawn shop.

I settled back and glanced around. Next to me in the seat, I saw a man in a dark tweed topcoat, white silk scarf, pearl-gray fedora with matching gloves,

CHAPTER TWENTY

and a raging expression that might have jumped up and kicked me. It was Manelli. I pushed my hat back on my head and looked up at him.

"Nice of you to offer me a lift," I said.

"Shuddup," he snapped at me like an angry bulldog. Then he caught himself and sat back and brought up a smile that was worth about as much as German war bonds. "It's a bad night, Garrett. You shouldn't be out alone. Something could happen."

"Lucky for me, you happened along."

He snickered. "You've been shadowed most of the night, wise guy. We would've picked you up at the hotel, only you came up with that little piece of baggage there." He nodded toward the house.

"So, you're looking after me now," I said. "What a relief. And just when I was starting to miss Frankie Bell."

His smile tightened. "Frankie was clumsy." He waved a glove toward the front seat. "Now these boys, they're top dollar. No mess. No loose ends. Right, Teddy?"

The one with the baby face and gun kept grinning and looking at me. Almost nothing moved but the toothpick. "Right, boss."

I looked back at Manelli. "You left a loose end at the train station tonight. Hit and run isn't very tidy."

He looked vaguely surprised. "I don't know what you're talkin' about."

"No? So you brought in the first team just for me?"

He looked at me sternly, as if I'd called him a dirty name. It crossed my mind. "You forgot your friends, Garrett," he said. "That wasn't good."

"You haven't been very friendly," I said, "knocking off Stevens and that kid at the motel. And leaving your girlfriend on my bathroom floor? Tsk, tsk. That wasn't friendly at all."

He made a wheezing sound. "I didn't do none of that."

"No? What about Frankie Bell? He was your friend. Maybe he did the killing for you."

He shrugged. "Like I said, Frankie wasn't smart. He was clumsy."

"Too bad. You must be running out of friends. But then there's still Halstead."

His jaw set quickly, and he frowned. "Who?"

I crossed my legs slowly, hoping not to disturb the toothpick in the front seat. "Sure, that's right," I said. "You wouldn't know an expensive Philadelphia lawyer representing the Chicago group that finances your club, one who made regular visits there with Charles Stevens."

His eyes narrowed. Then the empty smile crept up again. "All right, Garrett. I know him. So what?"

"So, nothing. Only you could buy a lot of killing with the kind of money Halstead's been lugging around."

His teeth came together hard, and his mouth curled into a snarl. "I told you..."

I didn't wait for him to finish, I just hit him with it. "Maybe he's coming after you."

His face filled with an ashen menace. "And maybe you'd better button it. You might just get buried."

"Uh-uh." I shook my head. "You need me alive. Besides, you haven't got anybody to do it for you except Abbott and Costello here." I nodded toward the front seat. "And they've already missed one tonight."

The one with the gun bit down on the toothpick. He raised the .38 a little and stared at me with a predatory calm. Manelli chuckled and spoke to him. "Relax, Teddy. It's not time yet." Then he turned to me. "Always the kidder, aren't you, Garrett. Full of jokes. Well, have your fun. The ride's almost over."

We cruised back through town and onto Mayfair and out through the fields and farms. The houses were all dark, minding their own business. The same dark elm trees stretched along the road, groping in the wind. I remembered Wells. I wondered if he was still in his office.

The Buick pulled to a stop at the curb. The Silver Club was dark except for a single light in an upstairs window. The two gunsels escorted me out of the car and into the club. I felt like the honored guest at a hanging. Manelli led the way, turning on the lights and opening the door in the far corner of the main room. His boys dragged me up the stairs, into his office, and slammed me into a chair in front of the desk. Then they took off their coats and hats,

CHAPTER TWENTY

parked them in another chair, and stood on either side of me, waiting.

After a very long minute, Manelli came into the office followed by Daphne Croft. She was wearing her club outfit and a knowing smile that I didn't like. Manelli came over, stood next to me, and motioned to her. "See, baby. I told you we'd get him."

She sauntered over and stood in front of me, her green eyes simmering. "Well. Hello, handsome." Her voice had the rough edges of anger. "I owe you."

"Why," I asked. "Did I get too personal?"

Her smile vanished. She made a sharp hissing noise, sucking in air. Then she quickly leaned forward and spat in my face. Manelli grabbed her arm and pulled her back.

"C'mon, baby." He looked over at me, pleased. "Save it."

"I owe him, Silver," she seethed. "I told you that. I owe him."

"Sure, sure," he said. "You'll get your chance. Now run along down the hall and wait for me." He guided her toward the door, giving her back a promising pat. She reached the door and stopped, and shot a long look back at me. Then she left.

Manelli moved over behind the desk, hung his coat and scarf over the arm of his chair, and carefully placed his hat and gloves on the shelf behind him. I slipped off my hat and trench coat and handed them to the tall character on my left. He flung them into the corner on the floor. Then he folded his arms, ground his teeth together, and looked over toward the desk.

Manelli was sitting in his chair, hands folded, eyeing me the way a starving man looks at a steak. "All right, Garrett," he said. "Where is it?"

"Where is what?"

He gave out a coarse laugh and reached into the upper drawer of his desk. He pulled out a small piece of paper and tossed it over in front of me. It was blue-lined notepaper with two columns of handwritten figures and a ragged edge, as if it had been torn out of something. I turned it over and looked at the back. There was a note scrawled in a childlike hand. It said, "*$100,000 if you want the rest of the book. See Garrett.*"

"That was slipped under the front door of the club sometime tonight," he said. "I mighta known you'd try to pull a cheap shakedown. I figure you got the book from the Tempest broad. Then you stashed it and decided to go into business for yourself."

I casually pulled out a cigarette, lit it, and blew the smoke at the ceiling. "What makes that book so important to you?"

"What the hell do you care?" he snapped. "Just don't think you're gonna get away with tryin' to put a squeeze on me."

I crossed my legs and blew a lungful of smoke across the desk at him. "I'm doing all right so far. Otherwise, I wouldn't be here."

He clenched his teeth tight together and spat at me through them. "Listen, you cheap gumshoe. I've had enough of your kidding around. I've finished off tougher guys than you for breakfast. Now, where's the book?"

"Suppose I told you I don't have it?"

A vicious smile started up the sides of his face. "Then my boys here go to work on you. If you're lying. I'll find out. If you're not, I'll find that out too…after a while. Either way, there won't be enough of you left to sell pencils on a street corner."

"Then suppose I told you I can get it?"

He eased back into his chair. "Now you're gettin' smart. When?"

"After we talk business."

He leaned forward abruptly, pounding both hands on the desk. "Don't push it, Garrett. You're damn lucky just to be alive."

"Listen," I said. "Thanks to you, I've been beaten up, sapped, and kicked around. I'm in a scrape with the law. They might still try to hang something on me. And I'm cold. I ought to have something for my trouble."

He reached up and scratched his chin. "Maybe you should at that. But don't think you're gonna get any hundred G's."

"How much, then?"

"Five," he said impatiently, "no more. Now, where's the book?"

"What's the rush?" I said. "Let's talk about it."

"Look, Garrett…."

"I'm not in any hurry." I stubbed out my cigarette in his silver ashtray. "Maybe I don't want to sell. Maybe I can get a better offer from Halstead."

CHAPTER TWENTY

Manelli's face took on the purple-gray look of a late-summer storm. He jumped up and came around the desk at me, and the two goons grabbed my arms. He used his open hand and slapped it back and forth across my face ten, maybe twelve times. After he'd hit me enough to get arm-weary, he stepped back and stood wheezing, short of breath, his jaw set as tight as a drill press.

My face felt like seared meat. I looked up at him. "Had enough?"

He raised a fist and stepped toward me. "Why, you…" He was about to throw the punch when a quiet ringing somewhere in the desk stopped him. He looked back, startled. "What the…."

He bounded over behind the desk, yanked open a lower drawer, and lifted a phone receiver to his ear. "Yeah? Hey, you're not supposed to be calling here anymore…I know. I know. You'll get it…. Look. With Stevens dead, we're a little behind…. No. No. Everything's under control…. Well, tell them not to worry…. All right…all right…. Yeah." He hung up.

Manelli stood up, put both hands on the desk, and leaned toward me. "All right, Garrett. That's it. You've caused me enough trouble. Now you're gonna tell me where that book is."

He looked over to the one named Teddy and nodded. Teddy reached into his pocket and pulled out a length of rope. The other man yanked my arms around behind me and held them while Teddy tied my wrists together.

I looked across the desk at Manelli. "We can still make a deal," I told him.

He grinned back at me. "Sure we can…after the boys work on you. I want something for my trouble too." He walked over to the door and stopped. "Give him a taste, Teddy." He turned and went out.

I looked up at Teddy. He was standing in front of me, chewing on the toothpick. "Suppose I save you the bother and tell you where the book is?" I asked.

"That's fine, pal." There was a gleeful spark in his eyes. "But it's no bother." His face broke into a grin. He took out the toothpick and pointed between my eyes. "I don't think you get the picture, pal. The boss wants us to give you the works."

So, they went to work on me. I'd been beaten up before. Each time was memorable. These two took turns. One would go at it while the other smoked or drank coffee. I passed out a couple of times. They would just revive me and start again. It became almost a dream. I saw only moving shapes and colors, blurred images. Light and dark were all the same. Time moved in slow motion.

Finally, it stopped. The two men put their coats on, and the tall one headed out the door. Teddy stood by the chair and put a hand on my shoulder. "Don't worry, pal," he said. "There's more." Then he left.

I don't know how much time went by. It could have been months. I sat there feeling as if I had just crawled out of a cement mixer. Most of the sensation in my arms was gone. My shirt was soaked in my own sweat, and a train whistle was raging in my head. I blinked and tried to move my arms. They weren't interested.

I was so busy trying to convince my arms they were still attached, I almost didn't hear the door opening behind me. She quietly closed the door and walked over in front of the chair. She stood there facing me, her muscles tense and her features as tight as piano wire. The smile was gone, but she still had that knowing look. I watched her. And I watched the knife she was holding. It was long and businesslike, and she held the point of it just inches from my chin. Then the smile started, and her green eyes glinted with amusement.

"It's time, handsome."

Chapter Twenty-One

I leaned back in the chair and breathed deeply, trying to clear my head. Daphne moved closer, the smile fading, her eyes intent. She traced the point of the knife along the underside of my chin and slid her left hand behind my neck. Then she moved the knife away and leaned over and kissed me. It was a serious kiss. I made the most of it. Finally, she pulled away and looked at me.

"Not bad," she said.

"I could get better, under the circumstances."

"I'll bet you could, handsome." She grinned and slipped the knife behind me. She leaned close again and moved her hand down along my back, positioning the knife. She placed her cheek next to mine and breathed, "I'll bet you could." She cut the rope.

She stepped back and put the knife down on the desk, and looked at me with a cool morning stare. "Mr. Garrett, I'm Sergeant Croft. I'm working for Lieutenant Wells."

"So, you're the one," I said. "What kept you?"

"I'm sorry. Manelli is just starting to trust me. I had to make it look real to keep him convinced."

I wriggled out of the rope and tried to rub the circulation back into my arms. "Where is he?"

"He went out. He said something about finding the book."

"What about his two hoods?"

She smiled. "I've taken care of them. They won't be any trouble."

"I'll bet you smiled at them, and they rolled over dead."

She laughed. Her green eyes gave me a wouldn't-you-like-to-know twinkle. "Now, don't be ugly."

My watch said eight o'clock. I went behind the desk and pulled out Manelli's telephone. I dialed the operator and got the number for Winifred Adams. Daphne walked quickly out of the room while I placed the call.

"Hello."

"Winnie, this is Garrett. Are you alright?"

Her voice had sounds of morning-after wreckage. "I think so."

"Can you meet me at the foundry in half an hour?"

"I...I don't have a car."

"Take a cab. I'll pay for it. Just be there in half an hour." I hung up.

Daphne walked briskly back into the room carrying my .38. She handed it to me. "I thought you might need this."

I tucked the gun into my belt. "So far, it hasn't done me much good. Do you have a car?"

She grinned and held out a set of keys. "It's a brown coupe, parked out back."

"Thanks," I said. "Call Wells and tell him to meet me at the foundry."

Her eyes clouded a little, and she put her hand up against the side of my face. "Are you alright?"

"I've been better."

It was a half-gray, cold morning. As I drove back through town, I noticed that the streets were mostly deserted. There was no traffic. The town was keeping to itself.

Winnie was waiting for me at the front gate of the foundry. She was standing there with a big man in a brown hat and trench coat. I got out of the car and spoke to Sergeant Moran. "Where's Wells?"

"Home. I was in the station and got the call from Sergeant Croft." He stretched out a grin that went halfway up around his nose. "What do you think of that, Garrett? A policewoman."

"Imagine that," I said. I started toward the gate. "Let's go in."

We went up to Stevens's office. Winnie unlocked the door, and we went

CHAPTER TWENTY-ONE

inside. The inner door was locked. She didn't have a key for that, so I borrowed a letter opener from her desk and jimmied the door. She looked horrified. Moran chuckled at me.

"You're a pretty good burglar," he said.

I went over to the desk and tried the top drawer. It was locked. Moran came over quickly and gave it a two-handed yank. He grunted, and his face reddened. But the drawer didn't move. I took the opener and started to work on the lock.

Winnie came over and put her hand on my arm. "Mr. Garrett, please. Not again."

"It's alright, Winnie," I told her. "Just stay out of the way."

I worked the opener back and forth until the lock snapped. Then Moran pushed me aside, jerked the drawer open, and shoved his hand inside. While he was fishing around, I moved behind him, brought my foot up to the edge of the drawer, and slammed it shut on his hand. He let out a howl that sounded like a wounded lunch whistle. I grabbed him by the coat and slammed him into a chair in the corner behind the desk. He fell over the chair and sprawled on the floor. I stepped back toward the desk, and he stood up, his face covered with surprised anger.

"Have you gone nuts," he blurted.

"I owed you that one." I had the .38 on him. "Now sit in that chair and behave. I haven't had a chance to shoot anybody with this thing since I bought it, and I'm in the mood."

He settled into the chair and rubbed his hand, and glowered at me. I glanced quickly behind me. Winnie was cowering by the door, her face filled with a pale terror.

"It's all right," I told her over my shoulder. "Don't be frightened."

I held the gun on Moran, and with my other hand, I carefully reached into the drawer. Toward the back, I felt something small, leathery, compact. I pulled it out and held it up in front of me. It was a small brown leather notebook. I thumbed through it using just the one hand. There were two small blue-lined pages, most of them with two columns of handwritten figures. And there was a ragged edge along the binding in front where a page had been torn out. I closed the book and slipped it into my pocket.

"That's evidence," Moran growled at me.

"Sure it is," I said. "And it's going to hang somebody. That's why you've been shadowing me all this time. You hoped I'd find this book. Then you could snatch it and take it to your boss."

I watched his face fill with a gloomy hatred. I sat back on the edge of the desk and looked down at him. "Something's bothered me about you from the beginning, Moran. It's the way you keep showing up, always on the spot. The night I first went to Shady Lodge, it took me a good twenty minutes to get there from downtown. Half of that was on the highway. But after I had Ralph call the station to report the killing, you were there in under ten minutes.

Moran's face was a mask.

"When you showed up in my hotel room after the girl was killed, I thought it was just coincidence. But then, when you called the station, Ferris and the lab boys showed up right away. I found out later that he had to make several stops first, that it was some time before he could get to the hotel. You must have called him before you even came to my room."

He opened his mouth to protest, but I just kept on.

"At the tailor shop, you were there just in time to keep Bell from killing me. You said Wells told you to shadow me. But Wells told me that he had you watching the Stevens house. And when you showed up at Ryan's last night, you weren't there to deliver any message from Mrs. Stevens. That was convenient. But you were there to pick up the money Halstead left and take it to Manelli. You sold out to him, Moran."

He sat clenching his teeth and glaring. I crossed one leg over the other and rested the gun on my knee, and continued.

"I think it goes this way: When Bell first spotted me at Ryan's with Mrs. Stevens, he reported that to Manelli. Then Manelli told you to tail me. But he had Bell tail me too, only making it obvious, so I'd be watching for him and not you. That was clever. That's why you got to the motel so soon after I found Stevens.

"You didn't know that Gloria Tempest was there at Shady Lodge then. And

CHAPTER TWENTY-ONE

you didn't know that Ralph was working for Wells. He hid the girl. He was sweet on her. And he was afraid for her, so he sent her to me for help. But he was still scared, so he told you later who he was and what he was doing. He must have told you where to find the girl and asked you to protect her. Then you panicked. You killed him and went to my hotel. When I left, you went into my room."

He glared at me some more and gripped the arms of the chair tightly.

"When I came back, you slugged me and planted the dope in my coat. Too bad it wasn't better stuff. That must have been your own idea too. I was supposed to be tied up downtown long enough for Manelli to find his book. Wells was supposed to think the girl had the dope and that I killed her for it. And I was supposed to think that Frankie Bell did it. I did think that too until I realized that if Bell wanted to give me a message, he wouldn't beat me up and then call me on the phone. So, after you hit me, you went downstairs and called Ferris and told him to round up the lab crew. He probably told you it would take some time. That was okay. I'd be out for a while."

Moran twisted around in the seat. "You can't prove none of this."

"It won't be hard to check with Ferris," I said. "But there's more. You didn't count on Wells seeing through your frame. And it didn't dawn on you that he might want me out on the street. It seems I was keeping everybody busy while he had somebody planted at the Silver Club, somebody who might recognize you. You didn't know about Sergeant Croft. Did you?"

The glare evaporated. He shook his head. "She couldn't have seen me. I mean...."

"I didn't say she did," I said. "But that idea bothers you, doesn't it? Well, you're going to love the rest. Wells didn't know about the book, but he figured Bell was out after something and that maybe he killed Stevens looking for it. So, he told you to watch the house. You alerted Bell, so he could sneak in and search the place and not tip your hand to Wells. But Bell didn't find the book, and Manelli was getting worried. He figured maybe I'd found it, so he sent Bell after me, and you after both of us. Bell was supposed to find out where the book was by beating it out of me. Then after I talked, you'd show up at Solomon's and put us both away. No loose ends. Bell was your fall guy.

But Solomon was still alive, so you couldn't plug me. That must have frosted you."

He bared his teeth and hissed at me. "You son of a bitch."

I shrugged it off. "But I didn't have the book either. I didn't even know what it was. Not then. And even then, I only had suspicions about you. It was after I saw what Halstead was doing that I started to figure things out. Then, when you walked into Ryan's, I knew. You were there for the money. You were Bell's replacement."

I waved the gun at him. "It's time to come clean, Moran. All this time, you've been a stooge for Manelli, giving him the word every time Wells tried to nail him."

His face turned as white as Solomon's chalk. He was ready to crack.

"You're going to fall, Moran. You're going to fall hard. This book will take Manelli down, and he'll take you with him. And you're going down for murder."

Now his eyes bulged wide. He shook his head.

"Oh yes," I said. "Manelli will try to give you up and let you sniff the fumes. You could have shot Stevens and Gloria Tempest. Your boss had the motive. You had the opportunity." He kept shaking his head. "And then there's Ralph. That was dumb. Wells won't stop until he roasts you for that."

His head stopped moving. His jaw began to quiver. "That wasn't me. It…it was Frankie."

"Was it? Bell would have used his hands. He didn't need anything else. And he wouldn't have gone at Ralph from behind, the way you have to when you're going to garrote somebody." I watched him. He sat there now, frozen, like a cornered animal waiting for the hunter's bullet. "No. You killed Ralph. Maybe you killed the others too. But it doesn't matter. Manelli will stick you for it anyway."

Now there was panic in his voice. "No…. No…. He can't. I didn't…. He can't." He licked his lips, his eyes pleading. "I won't let him. I'll talk. I'll turn state's evidence. Then they won't kill me, will they?"

"Maybe not. Who knows? Maybe they'll only execute you once instead of three times."

CHAPTER TWENTY-ONE

"No," he raved, "they won't." He was talking to himself now. "I'll tell. They won't kill me. I'll tell everything."

"Fine," I said. "Tell it to Wells."

I slowly reached into his coat and pulled out his service revolver, and laid it on the desk. Then I got his handcuffs out of his pocket. I looped his right arm through the right side of the chair and cuffed his wrist to his ankle. He didn't resist. He was like a big rag doll, limp and tired.

"All right, Moran," I said. "Where's Manelli?"

His eyes rolled around, and his mouth moved, but he didn't say anything. I shook him and asked again. His eyes finally focused, and he began to speak in a leaden voice. "He's at the Stevens house. Since you were there last night, he figures maybe you left the book with that dame."

I squeezed the corner of the desk hard enough to break it off. I went over to Winnie. She was still standing by the door, staring, her mouth open. I held her by both shoulders and forced her to look at me.

"Winnie, call Lieutenant Wells. Call him at home if you have to. Tell him to meet me at the Stevens house right away. Tell him Manelli's there."

She blinked several times. "Did he kill Mr. Stevens?"

"Just tell Wells to meet me there right away," I said.

She gave me a blank look and nodded, so I left her standing there and ran downstairs and out into the street.

Chapter Twenty-Two

I had left Daphne's coupe parked by the curb. I quickly got in behind the wheel, slipped the key into the ignition, and listened to the roar of a powerful engine. The coupe made better time than the DeSoto. I got to the house in a little under ten minutes. I drove past the house and around the block, so Manelli wouldn't hear me coming up the drive. I parked on a side street, the same one where Frankie Bell must have parked the day before.

I worked my way through the evergreens and went up to the back patio. The door was locked and bolted. I stepped back and looked up at the balcony above the patio. As I was looking, I brushed against one of the evergreens. It was still bent and twisted where Bell had jumped on it. I took hold of the good tree standing next to it and worked myself up enough to get a hand on the ledge of the balcony. I tore my trousers, scraped my shin, and finally made it up over the ledge.

The louvered doors were locked. I pulled out my investigator's ID and used the plastic casing to slip the lock. It took less than a minute. I stepped quietly inside and looked at the shambles that used to be the bedroom. Manelli hadn't missed anything. Even the mattress had been pulled off the bed. I waded through the dismantled room, stepping over bottles, shoes, and articles of clothing. There was a suitcase flung open in the doorway, and next to it a crumpled blue hat. I picked up the hat, pushed the suitcase aside, and went out into the hall. I listened. There was a sharp slap and a muffled cry.

I quietly made my way down the stairs. As I reached the bottom, I could hear Manelli's ominous wheeze coming from the drawing room.

"I don't care, lady. I'll take you apart too, if I have to. I want that book."

CHAPTER TWENTY-TWO

I did a fast soft-shoe number over to the front door and unlocked it so that Wells could get in. I didn't mind if Manelli heard him. Then I moved quietly back next to the doorway and carefully peered around the corner into the drawing room, my gun leading the way.

Manelli was standing with his back to the door, his coat off, his hair rumpled, and a .45 in his hand, leveled at Lenore Stevens. She was standing next to the sofa by the fireplace, arms folded tightly, her face a mixture of fear and loathing. She was wearing white slacks and a maroon sleeveless sweater that almost matched the red welt on her cheek. I recognized Manelli's handiwork. Lenore looked at him, her eyes smoldering. She held her teeth together and muttered at him with a throaty insistence.

"I tell you, I don't have it."

Manelli just stood there for a minute, wheezing. I took a deep breath, came up behind him with a couple of quick strides, and brought my gun down hard on his wrist. He yelped and let go of the .45, and turned toward me. I swung the gun again and brought the barrel sharply against his temple. He staggered over against the wall and brought his hand up to the side of his head, a trickle of blood starting down through his fingers and along his right ear. I kicked his gun across the floor to the right, out of the way, and turned to Lenore.

"Michael," she cried. "Thank heavens." She slumped down on the arm of the sofa and began rubbing her cheek.

"Are you alright?" I asked her.

"Yes. He slapped me a few times. That's all."

Manelli straightened up and began mopping the side of his face with a handkerchief. He looked angrily at me. "Garrett, you goddamn bastard. I shoulda had the boys dust you off."

"That was your play," I agreed. "And you missed it. Now we wait for the law."

He grunted. "You crummy peeper. I'm protected. The law won't touch me."

"You mean they haven't so far," I said. "How could they? They don't know what your game really is. Who would ever figure somebody using prostitution and dope as a front while laundering money for the Chicago mob?"

He leaned toward me with a menacing grin. "You got nothin'. You're just reaching."

"Maybe. But I've got pretty long arms." I gave him one of my best smiles and went on. "It started ten years ago in Philadelphia when you were a lieutenant for Anthony Petrone. You'd been that for a long time. You were tired of it. You wanted more. The old boy was getting ready to step down, and you expected to take over. But then you found out that he was planning on somebody else. Am I right?"

He stood there with a grim smirk. "Go on, shamus. You're the storyteller."

"Sure," I said. "You decided to move Petrone out yourself and take over. You connected with a flashy, good-looking businessman with something less than Boy Scout scruples."

I looked over at Lenore. She was staring at Manelli, jaw set, hands squeezed together. So, I went on.

"You and Charles Stevens became partners. In 1938 you sent him out here to Lancaster to start setting up the operation and to keep Petrone in the dark. Stevens bought the Wheelright Foundry with money you got for him from Ray Floren in Chicago through a phony company called Mid-States Development. Floren sent his boy Mannie here to keep tabs on the money, and you worked out the whole financial deal with him."

Manelli's expression remained fixed.

"The Chicago boys wanted somebody around who could keep an eye on things locally and who could keep their legal laundry clean. So they lined up Mark Halstead. He became the go-between. He worked out the deal for the foundry, and later, he became Stevens's personal attorney. With the business growing, he had to be here a lot. That way, he could keep running dirty money to you from Chicago, and nobody was the wiser.

"In 1940, Petrone was getting ready to name Stevens as his successor. That's when you made your move. You killed Petrone, or you had him killed. You even wiped out his whole family."

I looked at Lenore again. Her knuckles were white. Manelli just stood

CHAPTER TWENTY-TWO

there with a smug look.

"By then," I went on, "you had taken in a lot of the mob's money. And you were the only one who knew where it came from and where it all was. That was your insurance. As long as you were safe, so was the mob's money. They wouldn't dare touch you."

Lenore's gaze swung from me to Manelli and back again, as if she was at a tennis match.

"Everything went fine until after the war," I said. "That's when you started to have trouble with Joe Hinson. Then the Feds began poking around. You were afraid they might get to Joe, and through him, they might get to you. So, you decided to leave him in the cold. In 1946 you moved out here and set up your operation, making sure nothing could be tied directly to you. Your Chicago friends put together another phony company called Capital Investments Corporation. It was owned by Mid-States, so tracing the source of any funds would be even harder. And Capital Investments actually bought Shady Lodge and the Silver Club.

"But by then, you knew the law would be keeping an eye on you. So, you gave them something to watch. You started running a small-time prostitution-and-dope racket, and you spread around just enough local money to keep from getting shut down. But not enough to keep the heat off altogether. So long as the local cops kept after you, the Feds probably wouldn't bother. To them, you'd look like small potatoes. How am I doing so far?"

He kept on looking smug. He was good at it. "Pretty good, Garrett. Pretty good. But even if you're right, and I'm not saying you are, that's all ancient history."

"Keep your shirt on," I said. "I haven't gotten to the good part. Once you had your operation set up here, you wanted to make sure nobody could move you out the way you did to Petrone. So that same year, you had Halstead set up Stevens Associates, controlled by Mid-States again. And you had Stevens sell all his holdings to the new company. He balked a little, and Mid-States had to fork over more money than they planned. But you convinced them that was all right. After all, you and he were partners. And you had enough strings on him, or so you thought."

Manelli's expression soured a little, and he snorted. "Him. He deserved what he got."

I looked over at Lenore. She had a cold hard eye on Manelli. She didn't even try to conceal the hate.

"From then on," I said, "things went your way. Halstead kept bringing the money from Chicago. He'd have a place to pick up and a place to drop, like Ryan's. You'd pass the money to Stevens, using the lodge as a cover, and Stevens Associates would make the investments. By then, the money was nice and clean. All you had to do was collect the interest on it, take your cut, and send the monthly figures to Chicago."

He snorted again while Lenore kept staring at him.

"But then something happened. You got ambitious. You had ideas of setting Stevens up in politics. With him in the Senate, you could launder your money anywhere in the country. Only, Stevens was getting ambitious too. Now your partner wanted to pull out and take your would-be girlfriend with him. And he arranged to steal a book from your office. It was your ledger, your record of all the people you were laundering money for and where it was. Even coded, that book is dynamite. Without it, you couldn't give Halstead the monthly accounting. And Stevens threatened to use it to blow the lid off your whole operation unless you gave him his own piece."

Manelli's face was twisted into a scowl. The muscles in his neck bulged outward. "That bum," he said. "Friends meant nothing to him."

I didn't look at Lenore this time. I didn't have to.

"Maybe they meant as much to him as they do to you," I said. "But that brings us to the last couple of days. It was just one of those strokes of timing that the Hinsons got nailed and sent to trial at the same time Stevens made his move. And so, I showed up. You found out from one of your stooges that Stevens was at Shady Lodge, so you went there to get the book."

He thrust his jaw forward. "I didn't...."

"Don't bother," I said. "The girl saw you outside. And you left a calling card from your cigarette box in the room. You didn't find the book, so you figured Gloria must have it. But she'd made herself scarce. About that time,

CHAPTER TWENTY-TWO

Frankie Bell tipped you that I was at Ryan's talking with Mrs. Stevens. You knew I'd be looking for Stevens and, later on, for Gloria. So, you tried to hire me to find her for you. You didn't care about any money she took. You just wanted me to lead you to her. You probably even knew that I wouldn't agree to work for you. But just by trying to hire me, you made sure that I'd look."

The smirk edged back into his face.

"Well, that's one for you," I said, "because I did. In fact, I'm such a good detective, the girl found me. And she got killed for it. She didn't have the book either, so then you sent Bell out there, thinking maybe Stevens left the book with his wife. But Bell was clumsy. He got caught. He even got killed. You might have sent somebody else out here, but that's when the torn page was delivered. Somebody had the book who knew how to put on a squeeze. And you thought of me." I rubbed the side of my jaw. It still hurt. "What's more, you knew I'd be talking to Halstead. If I said anything to him about the book, word would get back to Chicago, and you'd be a dead fish."

His smirk soured. "But you told me you didn't have it."

"I didn't then. I do now."

His eyes widened. He clenched both fists at his sides. I looked over at Lenore. She had finally broken off her glare at Manelli. Now she was looking at me.

"So, where is it?" Manelli wheezed.

"In a place that's as safe as a bank vault."

He opened up his fists and warmed up his smile. "All right. How much do you want for it?"

"Why should I sell it to you?"

"Look, Garrett." A threat started creeping into his smile. "So far, I give you credit. You're a smart son of a bitch, smarter than I figured. Don't turn sappy now. I can set you up for life."

"Oh yeah," I said. "Whose life? Halstead is already suspicious of me. If he says the wrong thing, your life is worth about as much as yesterday's newspaper. And once the Chicago people finish with you, they'll be after me."

"I can take care of Halstead." He was still smiling.

"Maybe. But then you're forgetting the law. Lieutenant Wells wants to put you away."

"He hasn't got anything on me."

"You're right," I said. "But Sergeant Moran does." I watched the smile slip off his face. "And don't underestimate Wells. He might even try to tag you for murder. You had plenty of motive for killing Stevens and Gloria Tempest."

"I didn't kill anybody," he snarled. "Stevens was already dead when I went to the motel. And I didn't go near the girl. He can't pin those killings on me."

"Wells may not see it that way," I said. "But this time, you're right. He couldn't make it stick, because you didn't kill them."

Chapter Twenty-Three

The silence was like a clap of thunder. You could almost feel it. It came like an impulse, a stirring of desperation that reaches into your gut. It wasn't just the idle silence of people not talking or the preoccupied silence of someone waiting. It was the fearful silence of someone knowing that time has run out. I'd heard it before, too many times.

Lenore stood up. She wrung her hands together in agitation and looked at me. Then she pointed accusingly at Manelli.

"Michael, this is a nasty, miserable man," she insisted. "Of course, he killed them."

"No, darling," I said. "There was no sign of forced entry at Shady Lodge. Everything was nice and neat. And nobody broke into my hotel room. The girl simply opened the door. Charles and Gloria were both killed by someone they knew and trusted. That wasn't Manelli."

Manelli wrinkled his eyebrows and angled his head to one side. He was curious now. "What are you getting at, Garrett?"

"The real killer," I said. "Ralph, the kid at the motel, wanted to protect Gloria Tempest, but he was afraid that she actually did kill Stevens. He admitted to me that he saw someone who looked like her get into a car and leave at around three o'clock. You showed up at around five and left just before I got there. By then, Stevens had already been dead for some time. The blood on his shirt was dry. But Gloria told me that she was hiding in the main house. She saw you, she saw me, and she saw the cops. That means that she had to come back to the motel sometime after Ralph saw her leave. If she had shot Stevens, she'd have had no reason to come back. It doesn't make sense, unless Ralph really saw someone else.

"When Gloria came to my hotel the night before last, a kid on a paper route saw her go in. At least, that's what he thought. He didn't see her face. He saw a nervous dame with her collar up hustle in the front door. He didn't see anybody else. He just got on his bike and left. I saw him do that. I happened to be watching from the window in my hotel room. And Gloria was already there with me. She'd been there for some time. So, the kid couldn't have seen her.

"When the police showed him Gloria's body, that kid didn't know her from his great-grandmother. What he identified was her hat and coat. That's probably what Ralph recognized in the parking lot at Shady Lodge. It was a tan trench coat."

I turned and looked at Lenore. "Like the one I saw you in last night. And it was a plain blue hat." I reached under my coat and brought out the hat. "Like this one. I found this upstairs. When I first saw it yesterday, it just didn't seem to go with the rest of your wardrobe."

Her face was ashen. "Michael. What are you saying?"

"You killed Charles. And you killed Gloria Tempest."

She lifted her hands and then let them fall at her sides, her face clouded with disbelief. "Michael, that's the most ridiculous thing I've ever heard. It's not the least bit funny." She settled down onto the sofa and twisted her face in disgust.

Manelli put his hands on his hips, shook his head, and gave me a mocking grin. "Garrett, I think you've just gone fruity. She gets nothing out of this. Why should she do it?"

"You're right," I said. "She gets nothing. But that's one of the things about being a detective. You start to believe that nothing is ever quite the way it looks. You and Stevens were friends, partners, until something turned the partnership sour. You thought it was Stevens. You didn't know it, but you had another partner. A silent partner. Someone with a reason for wanting you dead. Someone with enough hate to squeeze you, bleed you dry, and then toss you to the wolves."

I looked over at Lenore. "You're very good, darling. But for someone who

CHAPTER TWENTY-THREE

didn't get along with her husband, who was used to having him away from home for days at a time, you were just too quick to hire me. He'd only been gone for two nights. What was so special about this time?"

She sat there, unmoving, her brown eyes blazing.

I continued. "I was suspicious from the start. But I didn't put it all together until last night, when I saw that picture of you and Charles. You were standing in front of a café in Philadelphia that I'd seen before, in another picture. It was the same café where Gloria Tempest started singing. A café run by an aging mobster." I motioned toward Manelli. "It was the same café where this crumb murdered the old man on the sidewalk and burned out his family."

I turned back to Manelli. "You made a mistake then," I said. "You didn't finish the job. Stevens wouldn't have opened the door to his motel room unless it was for someone he knew and trusted, like his wife. And Gloria Tempest wouldn't have let anybody into my room, except for the same reason. She wouldn't open the door for Lenore Stevens, or even for Lenore Parker. But she would for her old friend, Ellie Petrone."

Manelli's jaw dropped down to his belt. "My God." He looked toward the sofa.

Lenore just sat there in a frozen stare, her lips stretched tight and pale over her teeth as I spoke to her.

"You escaped the fire in 1940 and went out of sight. After a while, you surfaced out here with a new name, leaving nothing to trace. There's no record of Lenore Parker until 1943, when you married Charles Stevens. And you were careful about pictures. Charles wasn't the private person, you were. You didn't want anyone to spot you and then tip off Manelli."

Manelli was still looking at her, almost in admiration. "Ellie…Ellie Petrone."

She just kept staring at me.

"By then," I said, "you had already planned your revenge. It would take time, years. And you would use your husband to do it. That's why you married him. You knew how Manelli would set up his whole operation and how Charles would fit. You told Charles that when the time came, he could take over everything. He was more than willing. So, the two of you went into it together."

"Next, you decided to use Gloria Tempest. That involved some risk. You couldn't contact her yourself, because she'd recognize you. But she would have been a sucker for somebody like Charles. Your story about you and your husband not getting along was pretty good. It gave him a reason for being at Shady Lodge with Gloria. And you put on a good act for me, especially last night. But that wasn't enough. Mark Halstead and even your butler still saw you and Charles as the perfect couple."

By now, Lenore's eyes were trained on me like artillery. I went on.

"Finally, you had everything ready. You were going to bring Manelli down. But then Charles decided to run for office. You couldn't have that. It would bring you out in the open. So you nixed his plans. That made Charles angry, and he decided he didn't need you anymore. Maybe he thought he could handle Manelli on his own. Or maybe he really fell for Gloria. Either way, once the two of them had lifted the book, you had to eliminate them both. Then you spotted me. From what Ed Rawls told you about me, you decided I wouldn't be hard to fool. You could get rid of your husband and his girlfriend and leave me hanging between Wells and Manelli. That's why you killed Gloria with my gun. And that's why you put my name on the page you tore from the book. You had me all set up. It might have worked too, if only you hadn't tried so hard to cuddle up to me."

"You fool." Her words came out hot, bitter.

"I've been called that before," I said.

Manelli was still getting over the shock. "Ellie Petrone." He shook his head. "She killed them? She sent the torn page?"

"That's right," I said. "When I left Ryan's, she knew my first stop would be the foundry. That's when she went to Shady Lodge and killed Stevens. She dressed up like Gloria so that you and the police would think the two of them had a falling out. But she still wasn't sure about me. So, she burned up some marijuana and left it in the room to make it look as if Stevens doped himself up for courage and then shot himself. Then she went home and waited for me to come and break the news. She even pretended to faint."

I turned back and spoke to her. "That was a nice touch. Only Rogers told

CHAPTER TWENTY-THREE

me you had already retired for the night. But when I carried you upstairs, your bed hadn't even been turned down."

"The next afternoon, I came out here to visit the grieving widow. And you told me about Charles's affairs and how you had suffered through the marriage. You did that very well too. You even told me that your parents were delighted when you and he were married. But the marriage license lists your parents as deceased. So they couldn't have been too delighted."

She edged down into the sofa and didn't say anything.

"You knew then that I'd be looking for Gloria Tempest, so you followed me back to the hotel. As luck would have it, she was already there. You waited until you saw me leave, and then you went in and killed her. She must have been glad to see you after so many years. Her old friend. She wouldn't have suspected anything, even when you rummaged through my bag, found my luger, and shot her. But you shouldn't have shot her four times. That told me the killer was an amateur, not one of Manelli's people.

"After that," I went on, "you figured you were home free. But then yesterday, you found Frankie Bell in your bedroom, and you heard from Wells about the kid being killed at the motel. That frightened you. You needed a safe place for the book, so you went to the foundry. That was brilliant. Who would ever think of looking in an office that had already been searched? Too bad your husband's secretary happened to see you there. She told me about the lock being fixed. Then I started to wonder. Why would you want to collect keepsakes from a husband you didn't love? And why repair the lock on a dead man's desk? You hid the book there, except for one page. Then you went out to the Silver Club on the sly to leave the page with the extortion note. You got back here just before I arrived. That's when I saw the trench coat. And that's why you had mud on your shoes. You gave me a good story about almost being run down. You saw a black car, all right, Manelli's Buick. But it wasn't at the train station, it was at his club."

Finally, I shrugged. "You still might have gotten away with it, if you hadn't overplayed your hand with me last night."

Her mouth barely moved. "How could you do this to me? You really are a low-down bastard."

I shook my head. "Poor Eddie. He never knew how lucky he really was."

She looked sullen, her mouth twisted in contempt. "You can't prove any of it."

"You're right," I said. "I can't. But then, I don't have to. Manelli's already in hot water. There's a crooked cop who can't wait to squeal just to get himself off the hook. Once Moran spills, Manelli is finished. And the Chicago mob is going to lose a lot of money. When they find out it was Ellie Petrone who set them up, they'll come after you. And there won't be any place you can hide. That is, unless Manelli is willing to keep your secret. But I don't think you can count on that." I turned and looked at Manelli. "Can she, Silver?"

He opened his mouth to speak, then stopped abruptly. His eyes grew as big as poker chips as he stared at the sofa. I turned back and saw Lenore lift her hand up from between the sofa cushions. She was holding a small revolver, Stevens's other .32. It was pointed at my stomach.

"Go ahead," Manelli said. "Shoot him."

"Shut up," she barked.

Then she looked at me. "Put the gun on the floor." I did. "Now kick it over here." I did.

She reached down and picked up my .38 and held both guns on the two of us. Then she stood up and walked around to the end of the sofa by the window toward Manelli. She stood there looking at him, her eyes predatory.

"I wanted it to be slow," she said. "I wanted to make you suffer."

"Ellie," he wheezed, "what happened in Philly, that was only business. It happens all the time. Your old man understood that."

She hissed at him through clenched teeth. "You pig."

"Look, Ellie," he said. He motioned toward me. I could see beads of sweat on his forehead. "It doesn't have to be the way he said. We can be partners. We can go somewhere else. I can set you up. You can have anything you want."

She laughed. "Anything?"

His face brightened. "Yeah. Anything."

She laughed louder. "Anything at all?"

Now Manelli started laughing, a nervous laugh. "That's right. Anything

CHAPTER TWENTY-THREE

you want." He laughed some more. He was still laughing when she shot him.

Manelli staggered back and collapsed into a sitting position against the wall. He looked down at the blood running out of the hole in his chest. Then he looked up at me. His mouth opened, a little squeak drifted out, and his head slowly leaned over to the right and stopped. He sat there staring at me. He looked bewildered. He would wear that look for the rest of forever.

Lenore walked over and spat on him. Then she turned and looked at me, pointing both guns at my stomach again. "You were right about almost everything," she said.

"I miss a few now and then."

"Last night…."

"Last night was a fairy tale. I was Jack, you were Jill."

She waved my .38 impatiently. "For someone so smart, you can be awfully dumb." Then she sighed. "But I guess it doesn't matter now. You know I have to kill you."

I backed up a little toward the opposite wall. "That's foolish, Lenore. You can't get away. Wells is probably on his way here now. And there are still the people in Chicago."

"When the lieutenant gets here, he'll find you both dead. Manelli came here and threatened me. You, my noble detective, tried to defend me. You fought with him. But sadly, in the struggle, he got hold of your gun. He shot you. Then, protecting myself, I shot him."

I kept backing up. "What about the Chicago people?"

"They think I'm dead, that I was killed in the fire. I have enough money to leave the country and live comfortably. And you won't be able to tell anyone else about Ellie Petrone."

"But you can't be sure. I may have told Wells already."

"I don't think so," she said. "But I'll just have to take that chance, won't I?"

I took another slow step back. My heel came down on Manelli's gun. She raised the .38 and aimed it at my forehead. "Good-bye, darling. I'll always remember my gallant detective."

The first shot caught her in the abdomen, a smear of red welling on the front of her white slacks. She reeled into the corner against the bookcase, a look of surprise on her face. The second shot smashed into her side, just in front of her left arm, and the third shot tore into her neck. She was dead by now, but the shots kept coming.

Winnie Adams came through the doorway behind me and moved up to the end of the sofa, eyes wild, teeth gritted, saliva running down her chin. She emptied the rest of Sergeant Moran's service revolver into the lifeless form, now crumpled on the floor. When the gun was empty, she picked up a poker from the fireplace. Again and again, she crashed it down on what was left of Lenore Stevens.

And she kept yelling. "You killed Charles, you bitch. And you killed my sister! My sister! My sister!"

Chapter Twenty-Four

Wells walked beside me down the tiled corridor leading away from his office. The clicking of his heels echoed around us, making the empty sound of something deserted, distant. He shook his head.

"So, they were sisters. And 'Gloria Tempest' was her real name. She changed Winnie's name to protect her little sister. Doesn't that get you? And you were right about the clothes. Gloria was hiding in Winnie's apartment. So, it's no wonder Manelli couldn't find her. That dump is the last place anybody would ever look." He paused. "Do you think Stevens knew?"

I nodded. "Gloria was stuck on him. She trusted him. And he got Winnie the job at the foundry."

"But his wife didn't know about Winnie. You think maybe he really loved Gloria?"

I shrugged. "What difference does it make?"

Wells shook his head again. We kept walking.

"You were lucky," he said. "Winnie never called me. She just took Moran's car and went out to the house after you. She thought Manelli was the killer. You were really lucky."

"Yeah," I said. "I was lucky." I started buttoning my trench coat. "So, what happens now?"

"She's in an institution, a hospital. She's had a tough life, lots of problems. Not all physical. Gloria had become a mother to her, and she had started to think of Stevens as her father. When they were wiped off, it was like having both parents murdered. That pushed her over the edge. She'll be out of the way for a while. But if she recovers, I don't think any jury will touch her."

"What about Moran?"

He chuckled. "He's upstairs singing like a bird. With that notebook you found and what he's given us, we've already got enough to crack Manelli's operation wide open. We'll even nail Halstead and maybe some of the boys in Chicago." The furrows on his forehead crowded into a familiar frown. "But I'm not finished with Moran yet, not after what he did to Ralph."

He stopped and put his hand on my arm, and spoke quietly. "Are you going to talk to Rawls? I mean, about Lenore Stevens?"

"I'll talk to him...later."

"Something else," he said. "I always knew you were okay. But I couldn't tell you about Sergeant Croft. After what happened to Ralph, I just had to keep her protected. She had to play it the way she did so you wouldn't suspect. She wanted me to tell you that."

I didn't say anything.

"Oh, yeah." His eyes brightened a little. "One more thing. Solomon's out of the hospital. He's going to be fine."

I turned and started walking. We came to the front door and went outside. We stood at the top of the cement stairs in front of the police station and looked out at the street. A handful of cars rolled by, swishing through the road grime, flinging some of it up on the curb and not caring about the last three days. Wells shuffled his feet and cleared his throat

"Well, Garrett. I can't say it's been fun."

I looked out at the gray afternoon sky and turned up my coat collar. It was starting to rain again. Lenore Stevens was only a memory now, but one that would come back every time it rained.

"Just drive me to the train station."

About the Author

Richard Blaine (pseudonym) first wrote about Michael Garrett in the 1980s. As a part-time author, he also consulted with various companies and helped them produce documentation to enable staff members to understand how to use their computer systems effectively. Subsequently, Blaine went to graduate school and then became a mental health counselor, specializing in trauma and anxiety-based disorders. He had a very busy practice, lasting for twenty-five years, from which he then retired and returned to his earlier love of writing historic mystery novels.

CPSIA information can be obtained
at www.ICGtesting.com
Printed in the USA
JSHW021205070423
40065JS00003B/18